Somerset
Odyssey

ALSO BY LIONEL WARD

The Shakespeare Thief (Elliot Todd Mystery Book 1)
Roman Holiday (Elliot Todd Mystery Book 2)

Somerset Odyssey is dedicated to Marjorie and Ernest Ward, our mum and dad, sadly no longer with us, who were kind, generous and selfless, always supported us and scrimped and saved to give us holidays in the West Country, which inspired myself and Jo to eventually move there and where the story is set.

Somerset Odyssey

An Elliot Todd Mystery
Book 3

Lionel Ward

Onyx Publishing

Like one, that on a lonesome road
Doth walk in fear and dread,
And having once turned round walks on,
And turns no more his head;
Because he knows, a frightful fiend
Doth close behind him tread.

Samuel Taylor Coleridge, "The Rime of the Ancient Mariner".

Somerset is the county I live in (and love) and where the story is largely set. However, I have taken a few liberties. There are lot of references to the Coleridge Society though, in fact, there is no society called that in Somerset (that I am aware of) although I believe there is one of that name in Cambridge. There is a Friends of Coleridge of which I am currently a member. I have used the Coleridge Society name for simplicity and to distinguish it and its fictional members from the real thing. All the pubs mentioned are real but I may have taken a few liberties with the layout and the staff are all fictional. I have also taken liberties with the bus timetable to allow Elliot and Esther to take buses to places and at times when they may not in fact be currently available.

.

A letter had arrived at my bookshop, Ex Libris. It had become a rare enough event, to receive a letter rather than an email for something that was not a bill. It was from the Coleridge Society in Somerset. Both the address and the contents were also handwritten in ink. I wondered if it had been written with a quill pen and whether all Coleridge Society members still wrote using ink, sent each other letters and were against the very idea of the use of emails. I did hope so.

'The Coleridge Society want me to come and present them with the *Lyrical Ballads.*'

I shouted this to Esther, my friend, confidant and employee. She was on her knees, shelving some books in the biography section a little further along from where I stood behind the serving counter at the front of the shop. Now that she had finished, she pushed herself up onto her feet and walked towards me.

'Descending onto the people of Somerset from the magisterial Ex Libris Bookshop like a lord from olden days! I wonder if they realise it was stolen?'

She also had a wicked sense of humour – and a special place in my heart ...

In fact, *Lyrical Ballads* had come into my possession as a result of an encounter with a bookdealer in Rome. He had gifted the two volumes to me, but because of its uncertain origins I did not feel able to benefit from it myself and had decided in turn to pass it on to the worthy organisation that was formed to honour the memory and works of one of its authors, Samuel Taylor Coleridge.

'Not exactly stolen, but of indeterminate origin,' I clarified. I did not really need to explain. She knew perfectly well the situation, but I should make clear, for the uninitiated, that *Lyrical Ballads* was the result of an extraordinary flowering of collaboration between Coleridge and Wordsworth during their stay as near neighbours in the Quantocks. I was about to give the Coleridge Society in Somerset a rare and valuable early edition.

She continued in her playful mood.

'Now you are really beginning to sound like a lord. Do they know your wealth has been built almost entirely on slavery?'

'Oh, how do you make that out?'

'Well, Aggie and I work for you like slaves.'

Aggie was my oldest and original employee, close to but never quite achieving a state of retirement from the bookshop.

'You should make a proper holiday of it. I hear it's beautiful down there in the Quantocks.'

'I'm not sure if that would be fair. It's not long since I had one'.

'It was rather disrupted, and you had to fend for yourself while Cameron was in hospital - and half the time you were on the run.'

What she said was true. My trip to Rome with my history friend was full of incident, while at the same time there had been much to enjoy. Now that I had been granted permission to take another one (even though it was technically my decision to give myself permission to take this excursion, it would not happen without Esther and Aggie covering for me while I was away), my mind had already escaped the bookshop and was somewhere deep in the Somerset countryside.

Then a thought occurred to me. The contact with The Coleridge Society had inspired me to read up about Coleridge and Wordsworth and their time in the Quantocks. I had to admit, it was a fascinating story with obvious appeal to a bookseller and lover of English literature.

'Do you know what I would really like to do?'

'Run off with a local farmer's wife?'

'I was thinking I would love to walk The Coleridge Way, based on the walks that Coleridge used to take between the Quantocks and Exmoor. I was looking it up. It's quite a recent thing. 52 miles. Should be able to knock it off in two or three days.'

'Probably a more realistic option. And the exercise will do

you good. You are looking a bit pale and pasty and starting to develop a paunch.'

I ignored the jibe.

'They have this other thing now where poetry appears on an app when you pass a particular point in the Quantocks. I came across it when I was looking up the details of the Coleridge Society on Google.'

'Oh, very 18th century.'

'Actually, they were on the cusp of the 19th century when they were living there.'

She reflected for a moment.

'Yes, you're right. You're probably not aware of this, but I know quite a bit about the subject. I had to write a long essay about their time there when I was doing my degree.'

'Perhaps you can help me out with a bit of background?'

'Of course, there is much to learn.'

'Or even, you know,' I continued hopefully, 'you said after my last escapade you would not let me go on holiday without you again – to protect me from myself.'

'We all sometimes make rash promises on the spur of the moment.'

I had hoped that it was not a rash promise at the time she said it, but I was prepared to let it go.

What she said next, however, showed that she was still giving the idea of accompanying me some consideration.

'I think it would be difficult to get the time away,' she speculated. 'We can't really let Aggie run the shop on her own for too long. I know we have our student, but I think if it was more than a day or so… perhaps I could come down in the early morning one day, spend a day walking and go back the next day?'

'That might work,' I conceded. I was eager to keep the possibility alive.

'Well, we can work out the details of that later. For now, why don't you just say to them you can go?'

At that moment, customer and friend, Simon Bonneville, stepped through the door.

'Ah, two of my favourite people and together at the same time – my lucky day.'

Simon and I had been through a number of experiences

together in recent times. He was a tremendous supporter of our bookshop - and could charm the birds off the trees. He also periodically invited me to play for his cricket club that had recently acquired the name of The Bandits. Simon had become uncomfortable with it being known as simply Simon's Eleven. They were an informal mix of talented, indifferent and a few downright inept cricketers, some of whom seemed to be there just for the beer and camaraderie. The new name seemed to me to be a well-chosen one. They played most weekends throughout the summer. I could not make many games as they played mostly on a Saturday, when I was often required to work, as I was this coming one. I prepared to tell him that I could not make it this week.

But something else was on his mind that morning.

'Actually Elliot, I wanted a bit of advice,' he continued.

'Oh, yes,' I said, 'the new Robert Harris might suit you.'

'This is more of a non-fiction enquiry. I want to know more about trees.'

Esther gave a guttural scoff.

My small garden was an unkempt jungle. There were a few stunted trees in one corner, but I am not sure if I was able to identify any of them.

'I'm not sure if you have come to the right place,' I said. 'It's not my area of expertise. The garden centre is just down the road.'

'I mean a book on them and all the different varieties.'

'OK, I'm sure we can help you with that. Let's have a look, shall we?'

I began walking upstairs in search of our gardening and natural history section. He followed me and we began scanning the shelves together.

'I think I should also look at ponds and grassland,' he expanded.

'OK.'

This was typical of a conversation with Simon. He was not one of those people who laid all before you in a systematic way. I knew I just had to be patient. In time he would reveal all.

'I want to get involved...'

'Involved?'

'My garden is very nice…'

'Nice. It's stunning!'

I could attest to this having visited and had a meal there a few times at great potential risk to my personal health, given the amount of alcohol I had been persuaded to consume while I was there.

'The trouble is, it may look very nice, but it's not ecologically sound.'

'Ah, I see.'

His garden had a long stretch of lawn, beautiful flowers and quite a few trees. It was immaculately planned but there was not much wildness. I could see his point.

'I want to become self-sufficient in food as much possible - and go organic.'

'And perhaps a few chickens?'

'Yes, I was going to come on to that, and perhaps a pig to mop up all the bits of food waste. You know, something like a third of food is wasted – though not by me, I hasten to add.'

I believed this. Simon had always exhibited a healthy Churchillian appetite for food and drink. It was reflected in his figure, though at the same time as he was a little overweight there was a kind of energy and nimbleness about him that gave him the demeanour of a sleeker man.

During our exchange I had been forming a picture in my mind of the wonderful but long-suffering Miriam, happy amid a patch of vegetables but, unfortunately, after Simon's porcine utterance, an energetic sow entered the scene in my head and upended her as she was in the midst of pulling up some delicious baby carrots.

There was also another problem with the pig idea.

'I don't think you are currently allowed to feed food waste to pigs – not since that terrible outbreak of foot and mouth.'

'OK, I'll have to investigate that. I also want solar panels, certainly on the outbuildings. And I'm looking into a heat pump, perhaps even a windmill. We have oil, which is bloody expensive, so that might make economic sense anyway. I was even looking at one of those dry loo things. Might have a job persuading Miriam about that.'

'I think I know what you want. Let me see if we have one…

ah, yes, here we are, and a nice copy too. It's been reprinted several times over the years.'

I put into his hands a copy of John Seymour's *A Complete Book of Self-Sufficiency*.

'He was so far ahead of his time. It covers just about everything.'

I also sold him a second-hand copy of *The Tree and Shrub Expert* by Doctor Hessayon.

He left the bookshop in a buoyant mood.

'I knew you would be able to help me out,' he said to us both as he left. 'Best bookshop in the county.'

'Interesting,' said Esther after he had left. 'I didn't know he was that way inclined. Makes me like him even more.'

'Me too. I'm sure we'll hear a lot more about it in due course. Anyway, I'd better get back to the Coleridge Society and firm up the arrangements. I have the name and contact details of someone here called Jonathan. I think I will make a phone call. Always good to make a personal contact. I'll ring from the office.'

Jonathan was as friendly and enthusiastic about my visit as I had hoped – and about my decision to walk the Coleridge Way.

'I've done it myself with my wife. I think you'll enjoy it.'
He offered me accommodation for one or two nights.

'And don't even think about offering us anything for it. It will be a pleasure to have you.'

'Oh, thanks, that's really so kind.'

Isn't it wonderful how some people just make life so easy, I thought.

'Perhaps I could arrange to meet you at the other end of the walk?'

'That would be very nice.'

'Are you going to walk the extension?' he continued.

'Extension, I didn't even know there was one. Isn't 52 miles enough?'

'The extension is only just over a mile. '

'Oh, I guess I could manage that.'

'It's definitely worth it. I'm not really sure why they didn't include it when they extended the walk anyway.'

'I'm sorry, I'm a bit confused. I thought this was the extension?'

'When the Coleridge Way first opened it finished at Porlock. Then they extended it to Lynmouth.'

'So, this is an extension of an extension.'

'Precisely!'

'I see... I think.'

Over the coming days I began planning the details of my walk in the West Country. It would take place, I decided, over three days. Along the way I would stay overnight at two pubs. Jonathan would meet me at the other end. I would stay with him and his wife while attending the presentation and a Coleridge study weekend.

A guide to the Coleridge Way was available on the Visit Exmoor website with detailed instructions on each stage of the walk. I hunted out the two Ordnance Survey Explorer 1:25,000 walking maps that covered the route. I had always enjoyed maps, and we had an extensive selection in our bookshop. I spent some happy times over the next few evenings running my eyes and fingers along the route, examining in my mind's eye where the contours were closest together and, therefore, where the route was steepest and the best views might be had.

I had briefly discussed a charity aspect to the walk with Esther but quickly decided it was not a long enough walk to merit the charity title. However, against my wishes, word did get out about the walk thanks to a post on the Bookshop's Facebook page put up by Esther. I am not comfortable with social media (though I had found it useful in Italy when my friend Cameron had gone missing in Rome) but had come to accept that we could not really avoid it as a business as so many of our customers and potential new customers used it themselves.

Our bookshop hero walks in the footsteps of Coleridge and Wordsworth in his quest to return a valuable early edition of Lyrical Ballads to its spiritual home, I read during my daily perusal of Facebook, along with an old photo of myself walking that I did not realise Esther possessed. I sighed at the thought that in the photo I looked a much younger and fitter person.

'You didn't need to put my walk on Facebook,' I challenged Esther. 'I don't want the whole world to know. It's a private affair.'

'You can't really avoid it. People will ask where you are when they come into the shop. And besides, I'm not sure they will recognise the photo as one of you. It must be several years old and, I must say, it's rather flattering. They will probably think it's one of your student employees.'

I couldn't disagree with that, and she was right that people would notice my absence. One of the joys about running a bookshop over many years in a local community was the social aspect; knowing and developing a relationship with your customers in all their variety.

2

My visit was planned for the third week of August before the evenings became dark too early. I hoped that it would still be dry and warm. The Friday before my journey I received my usual weekly call from my mother, who had recently enrolled in studying an Open University course in Religion and Ethics. She had initially considered enrolling at the university which was local to me but had eventually decided the Open University gave her more flexibility. I was relieved as I may have been asked to give her accommodation during term time. Much as I loved my mother (I told myself), I also valued my independence.

As I was waiting for the call, I sat reading my current book, accompanied by a glass of wine to fortify myself. On this occasion it was a glass of chilled Pecorino for which I had acquired a taste from my visit to Rome earlier in the summer with my friend Cameron, the trip that had resulted in my unintended acquisition of *Lyrical Ballads*. I was delighted to find that it was available in my local supermarket (the wine not *Lyrical Ballads* - that would have surprised and depressed me in equal measure).

The book I was reading in preparation for my trip was Richard Holmes' first volume on the life of Coleridge, entitled *Early Visions*. It was a fine evening, a little cloudy and muggy but dry and warm, so I sat outside in my small garden jungle (save for the small patch of lawn I had mown to give me space to stretch my legs) and read on my garden bench. The space I had left for my lawn was even smaller than usual as I taken part in 'No Mow May' earlier in the year and a lovely patch of bright yellow Catsear (often mistaken for small dandelions) had grown up on one side of the lawn and a patch of daisies on the other. I could not bear the thought of mowing over them so, instead, reduced the size of the lawn further and had kept it that way. It made me think of Simon and his desire to become more environmentally friendly, though in my case, I reasoned, it was achieved more through idleness than sound ecological principles.

When my mother rang, later than usual at around eight-thirty, I was just beginning to think about moving inside. I was at the point in my book where Coleridge meets with Robert Southey (later to become poet laureate) having returned to Cambridge following a brief time in the army. He had enlisted in the 15th (The King's) Light Dragoons in December 1793 under the extraordinary sounding name of Silas Tomkyn Comberbache. Life, I was beginning to find, was never straightforward where Coleridge was concerned. At the end of his first year at Cambridge, he showed his developing poetic prowess when he won a medal for his Greek Ode but was disappointed in the second year not to win a classics scholarship. In the third year it seemed that the wheels had come off. He had developed an opium habit and was at the centre of an admiring student circle that put on wild parties. He left Cambridge in debt before the end of the autumn term. That was when he joined the army. He was eventually tracked down by his brothers who paid 25 guineas for his discharge. This enabled him to return to University for the Easter term, though he did not complete his degree.

But, back to the meeting with Southey. During the time of their meeting (at Oxford), both Coleridge and Southey were disillusioned young men with radical ideas, influenced as many were at that time by the French Revolution. They delighted in each other's company and conceived a scheme to set up an alternative community on democratic principles on the Susquehanna River in America. They gave it the name of Pantisocracy, derived from Greek meaning *government by all*.

This was all going on in my head when I answered my mother's call. We began by exchanging a few opening pleasantries. I had been working on these following numerous comments by Esther who thought I was not appreciative enough of my mother and considered I was often too impatient with her. I then explained briefly about what I had been reading and my forthcoming trip to the West Country.

'Actually, I will be in the West Country shortly for my New Religions project,' said my mother.

New Religions, I gathered, was the new term for cults. My mother was studying this as part of her university degree. Following the death of my father several years before and now 70, she had gradually been acquiring the education she had not previously had the opportunity to pursue. Like many of her generation, she had left school at 15, even though she was obviously intelligent and had an inquiring mind. I had to admit this, however infuriating I sometimes found her.

'Druids no doubt,' I replied. 'Will you be heading to Stonehenge?' I continued.

I could see her becoming pals with a couple of Druids. What if she married one? Do Druids even marry? I needed to check.

'No, it was a Christian sect... are you still there?' she said as I had not replied. I had been thinking about Stonehenge and my mother taking part in a Druid ceremony at sunrise.

'Yes, Mum, sorry I was thinking about something.'

'Something about your bookshop, no doubt?'

'Yes.'

How easily did I lie to my mother.

'I said not Druids, a Christian sect. It's at a place called, hang on a minute...' I heard the rustling of papers. 'Yes, here it is, Spaxton, in the Quantocks.'

'But that's where I'm going.'

My mother had always conspired, it seemed to me, to follow me around. On a previous occasion when she had stayed with me, she had become very chummy with some of the students at the local university – at least, those who frequented the student union bar. Esther had gone a long way to convince me that I was a bit paranoid about this, but now I was not so sure. I hastily glanced at my OS map that I had already open on a nearby table in preparation for my walk. I located Spaxton. Though it was in The Quantocks it was, thankfully, a little off the Coleridge trail.

All this time, my mother had continued talking away, but I had not been listening, distracted as I was finding where she would be visiting on the map.

'Sorry mum, I missed that.'

'Is your phone playing up again?'

It was always my phone, never hers.

'They were called The Agapemonites.'

'What?'

'They were called The Agapemonites.'

She was shouting down the phone, as though I was the deaf one.

'That's what I thought you said.'

I was still no wiser.

'The Community of the Son of Man.'

'I understand those words better, but it still means nothing to me.'

'It was based on the theories of German religious mystics. Agapemone means *abode of love* in Greek. There's not much to see apparently. I think it is a B and B or hostel or something now, but I can get a photo or two for my project and go to the heritage centre nearby to do some research.'

I rang Esther after we had finished our conversation.

'Typical of my mother encroaching on my territory like that.'

'Not really. She made plans for her project in complete ignorance of the fact that you were doing the walk. She could claim it was the other way round.'

As usual, Esther was taking my mother's side.

'When is she going? Perhaps you can meet up?'

'Thankfully, a few days after I come back.'

'There we are then, not encroaching on your territory at all.'

'I suppose not. Perhaps I am being over-dramatic?'

'Yes. But then all families have their strange dynamics, mine no less than yours. Reason seems to go out of the window where families are concerned.'

'I think of you as my reasoned interlocutor.'

'A part I am always happy to play.'

'But I mean. What are the chances?'

That was when she put the phone down on me.

3

I had one major task to complete before my trip to the West Country. I was to collect some second-hand books from a house a few miles out of town. It was a large collection from a local family, and I was not sure where we would find room for them in the bookshop. I had been putting it off for some time but the house in question was now sold and something needed to be arranged within the next few days. I had made a rough calculation based on the conversations I had had with the daughter of the owners (the father had died a few years before and the mother was now in a nursing home). I estimated that it would require at least nine or ten separate trips, if I was to use my car.

I related to Simon my problem when he came on Saturday to collect his book on installing solar panels.

'I might be able to help you there,' he said.

'I thought you were trying to shed yourself of books, not acquire more,' I said to him.

I had a few months before collected an impressive collection of *Folio* editions from his house.

'Well, you know, it's ironic you say *shed* books as, what I was going to say is, I do have a big shed, a barn that I could let you use. At present I keep my ride-on mower in there, but I can't see that I'll need it much soon, given that I'm going to considerably restrict the amount of grass I have – at least the lawn variety.'

'That sounds like a very interesting proposition.'

'The only thing is that there is no concrete floor. But I have some wooden pallets you can use that will keep the boxes of books raised off the earth.'

'Well, it could be the ideal solution. I've no idea where I am going to put all those books otherwise. My house and garage are already stuffed to the gills.'

'By the way, that self-sufficiency book you sold me is bloody marvellous. It just about covers everything.'

'I told you it would.'

'Of course, there have been quite a lot of advances since it was written.'

'Of course, inevitably.'

'You must come out and have a look when I have one or two of my projects underway.'

'Yes, I would love that.'

Just as Simon was leaving, the bookshop phone rang. I answered it.

'Hi, it's your historian friend,' I heard at the other end.

It was my good friend Cameron. In the last year we had managed two holidays together, one a biking trip in Kent and, most recently, a holiday in Rome. It had proved far more adventurous than we had intended and led to the acquisition of the copy of *Lyrical Ballads* that I was about to donate to the Coleridge Society in Somerset. It was unusual for him to contact me at work rather than in the evening at home, or at the weekend.

'Ah, you have some urgent historical fact you need to impart to me, no doubt,' I said to him.

History was his thing. He taught it and was now beginning to write about it.

'Better than that, I wanted to tell you about my new book that's coming out.'

'Congratulations, that's brilliant!'

I was genuinely pleased and had encouraged him along this route. He had cut back one day from his teaching role to find some more time for writing.

'There might be more. If the first one is successful, they may consider making it into a series.'

'You'll have to come to Ex Libris and give us a talk and, if we are lucky, we might even sell a few books. What's it going to be called?'

There was a pause.

'Actually, I need to ask your advice.'

'My advice! As you know I am more into the other kind of books – the ones you disparagingly call made up literature – rather than history.'

'But you do sell proper books – I mean history books - as

well. And have a wealth of experience about what sells.'

'I'm not sure if you are confusing me with someone else.'

'Well, be that as it may, what I would really like to do is run some titles by you – for the series, if it comes off.'

'OK.'

'Right. The first one. You ready?'

'Yes.'

'Right, here goes.' There was a pause for effect. '*History, the Best Bits.*'

'OK. Is that it?'

'Next one. '

'OK.'

'*History, the facts you didn't think you needed to know.*'

'Bit long - but I can see where you are coming from. How many of these are there?'

'Quite a few.'

'Why not say them all together? As you know, I am a busy man.'

'Yes, I thought I detected the rustle of an opened packet of biscuits.'

'Not right on this occasion. I am trying to give the little blighters up.'

But it was true. I did have a penchant for digestives and had been known to go through a complete packet in one afternoon.

'Alright then. *Disgusting History, Despicable History, Dastardly History, Devastating History, History Back to Front, Bonkers History.*'

'I think I like the last one.'

'You're sure that's not a statement of your prejudice?'

'Certainly not!'

'There are a couple more… *Baleful History* and *Crap History.*'

'*Crap History.* Really! That doesn't sound very Cameron – and, of course, it could be misunderstood.'

'I think it's an attempt by the marketeers in the publishing world to be *on trend.*'

'Are you sure you're my friend Cameron? I feel I've moved into some surreal parallel world. I never thought I would hear you uttering phrases like that.'

'Sometimes you have to evolve with the times.'

'Or that! Anyway, I'll have to think about them and get back to you. Perhaps you could email them to me?'

'Will do.'

'When is the book due out?'

'In the spring.'

'As soon as you have a firm date, we must set something up at the bookshop. You can come down for a few days if you like.'

'Yes, I'd like that.'

'Before you go, have you heard of a Christian cult called the Agapemonites?'

'Yes, it rings a bell. They were quite a thing at one time. Weren't they based somewhere down in the West Country?'

I then shared with him the details about my impending trip. He had known about my decision to pass *Lyrical Ballads* to the Coleridge Society and had given his blessing, involved as he was with the circumstances that led to my acquiring it in the first place. And then, of course, I had to explain about my mother's trip and her researching cults for her project.

While I had been talking to him, I had heard the unmistakable sound of Cameron tapping away on the keyboard of his computer.

There was a pause while I waited for him to respond. I knew that he had been researching the Agapemonites while we talked.

'Yes, here we are. The Abode of Love in Spaxton. What a quaint name for something that appears so insidious. You know, this chap Henry Prince, he preyed on rich ladies to fund his cult. Quite incredible really. He earned enough money to build a church in Clapham, The Ark of the Covenant. Actually, looks rather nice. He took what he called "spiritual brides". There is even some suggestion he may have engaged in a sexual act with a young girl as part of a religious service.'

'I don't think I want to know any more. Do you think my mum will be safe?'

'Oh, it's long gone. Having said that, it's extraordinary how long it lasted. From 1846 to 1956. Ah, I see, there were two of them. As soon as Henry Price died, one of his followers, Smyth Pigott declared himself as Christ reincarnated and became the cult leader. People are so gullible. He died in

1927, but it looks like it floundered on into the 50s. Some kind of bed and breakfast or a hostel now. Ah, look at this, they made children's programmes for the BBC there, *Camberwick Green* and *Trumpton* in the 1960s for a while.'

'I remember watching those.'

'I do too. Must have repeated them unless we are both much older than I thought.'

'I'll check it out.'

'I can quite see why she's interested in it for her project. Looks fascinating.'

At that moment a customer came through the door and behind him a girl in Royal Mail livery arrived with a parcel.

'Cameron, I've got to go. I will let you know about those book titles.'

4

I had arranged to meet Simon the following morning on the way to view the books that I would be collecting.

He was already waiting for me as I parked and led me over to a large black barn that was set in a field to the right-hand side of the house. It was unremarkable to look at, but, when we opened the door, I marvelled at the space.

'I could put my whole bookshop in here,' I said.

'But not its character.'

'Nevertheless, it would help me out enormously. What sort of rent?'

'Nothing. And that's not negotiable.'

'You're too good to me.'

'Nonsense, it's the other way around. Look how you're helping me with my project.'

'In that case, I accept your generous offer.'

'You can start moving stuff in whenever you like. Fancy a coffee before you go?'

'Yes, I'm running early for once in my life. My appointment's not for another hour.'

Simon phoned ahead to Miriam as we walked back to the front of house. Miriam met us on the front terrace with a tray of coffee and biscuits.

'I thought it was just about warm enough for you two to have your coffee on the terrace. And it keeps you out of my kitchen. I want to mop the floor.'

'You're not joining us then, Miriam?'

'I'd love to Elliot, but I have too much to do. Could you do me a favour and help finish off this shortbread?'

'I bet it's homemade!'

'Of course!'

'And, no doubt, made with organic flour.'

'Yes.'

'Your own?'

'Don't give him more ideas.'

Simon and I sat down and luxuriated for a few moments in the quiet and pleasant morning sunshine.

'You know what's missing Simon?'

'What?'

'The sound of chickens clucking.'

'Yes, you're right. Hopefully that will change very soon.'

I took a gulp of coffee and bit on a piece of shortbread.

'Great coffee and this shortbread is the best. You're a lucky man, Simon.'

'I know.'

We sat amicably in silence for several moments before he continued.

'So, this trip to the West Country, to the Coleridge Society, I think you said. I never did get to the bottom of what it was all about with this *Lyrical Ballads* book. It seems that rather than profiting from it yourself you are giving away a valuable first edition.'

'It depends on what you mean by the first edition. It's the 1800 edition but it isn't *the* first edition. That was in 1798. So, in fact, this is the second edition. There are several changes from the earlier one, but one of the main ones is that "The Rime of the Ancient Mariner" has been moved from the front to near the back of the book and Coleridge has made some of the language less archaic. Wordsworth objected to the old words and the strangeness of it and thought it damaged sales by having it as the first poem...'

'That's hard to believe when it is such a well-known poem. A great poem I would say.'

'Yes, hard to believe now but I think it was considered quite experimental at the time. I suppose the other big difference is that Wordsworth expanded his famous preface.'

'It's surely unusual for a preface to be famous. I often skip them myself.'

'It's now considered as the manifesto of the Romantic movement.'

'Whatever that is.'

'Before the Romantics you had the Neoclassicist poets who were more about reason and order. A bird's flight would be described as a controlled dance of wings whereas the

Romantics would talk about its soaring untamed spirit. For Romantics, emotion was more important than action or plot.'

'So how much is this book worth?'

'Three to four thousand at current prices. The original edition would be more than double that.'

'But still a valuable book.'

'Yes, and valuable in its content in that it is distinct from the first edition.'

'Now, I do know you have a reason for passing it on, but I must admit I don't fully understand the circumstances.'

'I was given a copy by a book dealer I met in Rome, Antonio Cantalbrini. I wasn't fully aware of it at the time, but I now think it was on the understanding that I would remain silent about his relationship with Mr Abruzzio. He died in the lift near the apartment where we were staying in Rome. There's no absolute proof of this, but it looks like he may have been murdered on his way to see me. I found him bleeding to death on the stairs that led to our apartment.'

'How extraordinary! Why do you think he was coming to see you – or might have been coming to see you?'

'Alessandro, the policeman, thinks that he may have been about to confess to me – or at least to ask my advice.'

'No disrespect, but why you, of all people?'

'I was with him and Cantalbrini at the opera the night before. I had this very intense conversation with him when Cantalbrini left us to buy some drinks. He was talking about corruption in Italy, and I think, on reflection, he was close to confessing to stealing books from the library where he worked. We later found out he was trying to raise money to send his daughter for treatment in America. She has a rare form of cancer. It led him, we think, to smuggle out valuable books from the library and change the inventory. I believe he was an honourable man who was put in an impossible situation. He was prepared to steal books but only to save his daughter's life.'

'Put like that, which of us would have done anything else? And I guess this Cantalbrini was the recipient of the stolen books?'

'That's what the assumption is. The challenge is to find a link between Abruzzio and Cantalbrini. Unwittingly, we were provided with evidence on the very first night we were in Rome. Cantalbrini was sitting at a table nearby. That's how we met him. He was very friendly and talked to us during and after the meal. At one point, though, he was joined by Mr Abruzzio, who showed him a book which, looking back on it now, may very well may have been a stolen one. That was why we believe Cantalbrini gave me *Lyrical Ballads*, to stop me passing on that information to the police. It was too late, in any case, as I had already spoken to them. He also did not want me to mention the opera visit as it would indicate that he was closer to Abruzzio than he would wish to appear.'

'Tricky situation for you.'

'The other bit that I haven't told you is that I found Abruzzio's phone at Cantalbrini's flat when I went to visit him. I managed to smuggle it away. It may have provided enough evidence to convict him. Unfortunately, Cantalbrini realised I'd taken the phone, and he and his friend chased us. I dropped it while I was running away from them.'

Miriam appeared with another pot of coffee.

'I thought you may want a top up.'

'I think we do, with what Elliot has just told me.'

'Oh, I'm sorry, Elliot. Not bad news I hope?'

'Just something that happened on my holiday in Rome.'

'I'll explain later, dear.'

'I'll get back to cleaning my floor.'

'And what's the latest on the situation?' continued Simon once Miriam had gone.

'I contacted Laura, a friend of Cameron's who has an important position at The Library Service, including preventing library thefts. She has a close relationship with Alessandro, the policeman we were dealing with. They think they do not have enough evidence to link him directly to the murder. However, stealing books is considered a serious crime in Italy. They are working on establishing whether any of the books in Cantalbrini's library are stolen ones. Even if some of them are it may be difficult to link him to Mr Abruzzio.'

'Didn't they want the copy of *Lyrical Ballads* back?'

'I suggested to Laura that I send it back to Cantalbrini - or the library it was stolen from. But Laura couldn't find any evidence for missing copies from any of the Italian libraries. There's a stolen books database and it doesn't appear on there. It was Laura who suggested I donate it to the Coleridge Society. She thinks only some of Cantalbrini's books will have been stolen, albeit some of the more expensive ones. These more expensive books allow him to buy legitimate ones and expand his business.'

'So, the police may not be able to prove anything at all.'

'That may be the result, but at present I believe he is officially suspended from trading, which I'm sure he's very annoyed about. I also believe he's not supposed to leave the country at present.'

'That's a relief for you.'

'Yes, I wouldn't have put it past him to give me a visit.'

'Well, it seems to me, you are doing the noble thing - and I wish you well with it.'

'I must admit I'm looking forward to my trip, especially the walk. To be honest, I'll be quite pleased to have the book off my hands. It will help salve my conscience.'

From Simon's I went on to the house from where I was to collect the second-hand books. I met Gina who was standing in the doorway at the front of the entrance to the house, framed by a beautiful arching spray of red roses.

'It's very good to meet you,' I said. 'I remember your parents as customers.'

'Yes, they loved your bookshop and made a particular request that you should have the books.'

'That's very kind of them. I enjoyed seeing them when they came in to buy books, though, when I hadn't seen them for a while, I did wonder. I thought perhaps they had moved away.'

'I think Mum never recovered properly once Dad had gone.'

'I'm sorry, you were obviously very close to them.'

'Yes, they were good people.'

A little tearful, she walked a few steps along the hall.

'Perhaps we'll start in the obvious place. The library is through here.'

I followed her into a large room, a library which also seemed to serve as a dining room. There was a long imposing ancient-looking dining table.

'A lovely room,' I said.

'Yes, it was great for our family gatherings. I especially think fondly of it at Christmas time when the fire was lit. It always had a lovely atmosphere.'

'What a perfect combination,' I said, 'books and food – and no doubt some wine flowed.'

'Yes, they enjoyed their wine. I'm afraid this is just the beginning, though. Nearly every room has shelves of books in them.'

She gave me a tour of the entire house. Every room, every bedroom, the lounge, ante room, kitchen and, even the downstairs loo, was full of books.

'They must have travelled a lot,' I said as I observed books on China, Egypt, Israel, Italy, France, Germany and the Baltic Countries in a small study tucked away beyond the kitchen.

'Yes, they did. But in lots of ways, I think they were happiest at home, travelling the world through their books.'

She smiled at the memory.

'Such an extensive collection. I think I might have to hire a van, otherwise I will be going backwards and forwards all day.'

'Where are you going to put them all?'

'That's a very good point. I have just been offered storage space by a friend of mine. As you will appreciate, it takes time to sort everything.'

'I'm afraid we don't have a very long time to sort it all out. The house has already sold even though it's only been on the market for a few days.'

'I'm not surprised. It's such a lovely house.'

'If you could do something in the next few days that would be amazing.'

I went back to Simon.

'No problem at all. Start using the barn whenever you like. You know I could help you. That's a big job you've got there.'

I must admit I was already finding the thought of the task a bit daunting and really, I had nobody else I could call on at that moment.

'That would be great, if you're sure?'

'In fact, I might be able to help you with a van. Let me make a few phone calls before you go hiring one.'

I drove back to the bookshop. I had only been there for a few minutes when Simon was on the phone to me.

'Just thought I'd let you know I've got it all sorted. I've arranged for a van, and it's registered in my name so I can do the driving.'

'Where did you get it from?'

'A friend of mine. It's all legit.'

I wasn't thinking that it was illegitimate for a moment. More likely, I thought, he had gone to a van company himself and taken it upon himself to make the hire.

My recent conversation with Simon about the circumstances of my acquiring *Lyrical Ballads* put me in mind of Laura again.

When I had returned to the UK with it in my bag several weeks before, I had phoned Laura and asked her what I should do. The conversation had gone like this.

'I took the book with me. Cantalbrini must've known I was not supposed to take it out of the country without an export licence.'

'He may have been thinking that once you arrived with it safely in the UK, he could perhaps charge you for it.'

'In our conversation, he definitely said it was gifted.'

'I guess there were no witnesses?'

'No. He did make a lot of the fact that we could help each other. I had no idea about how strict Italian laws on exporting books are. We only send a few books abroad from our bookshop and usually they are new or recent titles. I feel uncomfortable breaking the law.'

That was when she checked the international database of stolen books and, when I said I was uncomfortable keeping it, suggested giving it to a worthy society and went on to suggest the Coleridge Society in Somerset.

'In that way, she said,'you can claim that you are not benefiting financially in any way from the transaction.'

Now, a few weeks after that conversation and with my impending trip to Somerset, I decided it was a good moment to re-establish my contact with Laura. I gave her a quick text asking if there had been any development with regard to Cantalbrini and making her aware of my plan to go ahead with my visit to the Coleridge Society.

Moments later she rang me back.

'Ciao,' she said. 'I'm glad you are going ahead with your plan. I think it's the best thing.'

'I suppose so. I am still feeling a bit guilty about the fact that I've illegally taken out a book that is more than 70 years old without an export licence.'

'I've been checking the regulations. Here is the relevant paragraph. *Export regulations apply to any work of art in Italy, but not to those works that, although are currently in Italy, were produced abroad.*'

'That's a relief.'

'Yes, well, you're right to be worried. The illegal export of cultural works from Italy carries a sentence of between two and eight years and a hefty fine. I think what you are doing is the best in the circumstances. If it was stolen at some stage, there's a kind of justice that it's going back to its original home.'

'Do you know what's happening with Cantalbrini?'

'From what I have heard from Alessandro, it appears that they can find no direct link to the murder of Mr Abruzzio but they are hopeful of finding a link to stolen books - and book theft, as I think I have told you, is considered a very serious crime in Italy. The thefts from the Girolamini library in Naples that I told you about, where thousands of books were stolen, has cast a long shadow. The prosecutors have focused a lot on rare book dealers and collectors so he is very much in the spotlight.'

'It's such a shame. He's such an intelligent guy and very knowledgeable about books. Surely, he can make a living from legal means.'

'I have to admit I have some sympathy with book dealers and the strict rules with export licenses but the abuse and corruption with regard to our cultural heritage over the years has not helped.'

'And you have so much of it.'

'Do you mean corruption or cultural heritage?'

'Both, I guess.'

'Anyway, on a lighter note, I'm hoping to come and see you guys in the next few months.'

'That would be great. You'd be very welcome. You could stay with me – or Esther – and, of course, there is always that Cameron guy.'

Cameron and Laura were friends from university when

Laura studied for a year at Manchester. There had been a heated discussion when they were in Italy about whether Laura should visit me in the west or Cameron in the east of the country.

We were, in fact, able to begin emptying the house of books the very next day. We started at 8 am. It took five return trips, and we didn't finish until 9 pm that evening.

The variety of books was astonishing, and I was thankful that I had Simon's help - and the van. When it was clear that we would run out of boxes, Simon kindly went to the local DIY Centre and found some large plastic boxes with lids, particularly useful in case of any ingress of moisture while the books were being stored in the barn.

It was while we were sitting down for lunch in the back garden, eating sandwiches prepared by the thoughtful Gina, that Simon brought up something that was on his mind.

'I'm going ahead with my self-sufficiency project. I've been gathering lots of information and I've sought some professional advice.'

'That's good.'

'The thing is, while I have done all that, there are times when I just need a friend that I can contact to talk some basic things through.'

'Well, I'm always here for you to have a chat.'

'Someone, for example, knows a thing or two about actually growing vegetables. You know, the basic things. Is that something...?'

'No, no expertise at all, I'm afraid.'

I had a guilty moment thinking about my late father who did have green fingers and had gone to the trouble of trying to pass them on to me. Each of us children had our own little patch of garden. He had encouraged us patiently, first to grow sunflowers and then a row of peas, followed by potatoes and magnificent towering rows of runner beans. I remembered this time fondly and of being particularly proud of some peas that I harvested from our garden and experienced the joy of opening the green pods and 'shelling' peas straight into a saucepan ready for Sunday dinner. But I had not continued to grow anything much in the vegetable line in my own garden as an adult. I felt I had let him down.

'What about your Esther?'

Not my Esther, really, my work colleague and friend, but I did not try to correct him.

'She may grow one or two things, though I'm not sure that she would count herself as an expert either. I can ask her... but I will tell you someone that is.'

'Who?'

'Aggie. She's forever bringing runner beans and courgettes into the shop – and apples, now I think about it. She may be the sort of person you can chat to about vegetables and orchards. Shall I ask her on your behalf?'

'Yes, it may be better than me blundering in. Then she'll have time to think of an elegant way of saying no if she thinks it's too tiresome. And what about chickens? Does she know anything about them? Presuming you don't, of course.'

'Well, if we're talking chickens, I have no hesitation in suggesting Esther – unless you're suggesting doing battery farming in which case she will be down your way with a pair of wire cutters.'

'No, quite the opposite.'

'You know all her chickens have their own names.'

I would expect nothing less from Esther. I also intend to name my chickens individually.'

'In which case, I'll ask her as well.'

'It will be nothing too onerous, you understand. The trouble is, these professional people sometimes don't give you a straight answer and sometimes I'm too embarrassed to ask about the simplest things in case they think I'm an idiot.'

'I find that hard to believe.'

'What if I were to invite Esther and Aggie for lunch or afternoon tea - along with yourself of course?'

'I'm sure they would love that. Remember, though, I'm going away in a few days time. There's no reason why we couldn't book a date now, I suppose, for after I come back.'

'How about two weeks on Sunday? I can check with Miriam that it's OK with her.'

'I'm pretty sure I'm free. I'll check with the others.'

Alighting from the train at Taunton Station *en route* to the beginning of The Coleridge Way in Nether Stowey, I plotted a route diagonally across the town passing the cricket ground. Castle Way, from where I would take the bus for the next stage of my journey, was close to the museum, located in the twelfth century hall of Taunton Castle. I was drawn to the prospect of seeing the museum but also wanted to see the Mary Street Unitarian Chapel where Coleridge had preached. I had arranged to meet Denise at 8.30 am, a member of the congregation there. The early times suited us both as she had to go to work at nine, while I also wanted to leave myself a chance to have a quick look around the museum. I approached via the pedestrianised High Street, turning left after I crossed the road at the gates to Vivary Park. She was there waiting for me at the entrance.

'We Unitarians are part of the dissenting tradition,' she explained as we entered the church. 'It's always been very strong in Taunton. It was very much against the orthodoxy of the day. You know, Unitarian worship was not legalised until 1813.'

'I don't count myself as having any particular religion, I'm afraid.'

'That's all right. We welcome all here. We'll not tell you what to believe in but support you to explore your spirituality in your own way.'

'Sounds very accommodating. I'm particularly interested in the fact that Coleridge preached here – as you know from my email.'

'Yes, he preached here several times, but he is particularly remembered for the time when he walked 12 miles from Nether Stowey to take the service for Joshua Toulmin, the minister here at the time.

'Yes, I recollect reading about that.'

'In which case, you're probably aware that he was preaching for him because of a personal tragedy. His daughter had drowned in the sea at Beer.'

'Yes, poor man.'

'Some say that she committed suicide as a result of persecution of the family. Toulmin suffered severe criticism for his radical views, in particular for his support of the American Revolution and Thomas Paine's *Rights of Man*. He was often insulted in the streets and, one night, an effigy of Thomas Paine was burnt outside his house.'

'He sounds enlightened to me.'

'He was a remarkable man in many respects. As well as preaching here for 39 years, he wrote numerous articles and books, including the first history of Taunton - and he was the first person to conduct a census of the population, single-handedly visiting each house.'

'He does indeed sound like a very remarkable man. What about the chapel itself?'

'The current building was built in 1721. It was modified on the outside in later years but much of the interior is as it was when it was built.' She pointed. 'Such as those oak pillars and the pews and the pulpit.'

'So, it is very much the same as when Coleridge gave his sermon all those years ago?'

'Yes, though I guess the congregation may have been a bit bigger than we get nowadays.'

I wandered over to the pulpit. It was very imposing, standing high and proud at the centre of the chapel.

'Why don't you stand up there?' she said. 'It's not out of bounds as in some churches. In fact, we encourage guest speakers to our services.'

I ascended the stairs to the pulpit.

'That Bible you see there, it's the very same one he would have preached from all those years.'

'Really. It gives me goosebumps to think that.'

I turned some of the pages then looked out over the empty stalls trying to construct in my mind a late eighteenth century audience hanging on my every word.

'It's quite an empowering feeling standing up there, isn't it?' Denise said.

'Yes, it is. Do we know what he preached that day?'

'Sadly not, but there is a record of what he preached at Shrewsbury when William Hazlitt walked 10 miles to hear Coleridge preach. Coleridge got around quite a bit, as you probably know. Hazlitt was much impressed by him. He said his voice *rose like a steam of rich distilled perfume*. Make of that what you will. Here is the text of what he said. I prepared it, knowing that you were coming here. She cleared her throat.

'This is what Hazlitt said:

The sermon was upon peace and war; upon church and state, not their alliance, but their separation – on the spirit of the world and the spirit of Christianity, not the same, but as opposed to one another. He talked of those who had "inscribed the cross of Christ on banners dripping with human gore." He made a poetical and pastoral excursion – and to show the fatal effects of war, drew a striking contrast between the simple shepherd-boy, driving his team afield, or sitting under the hawthorn, piping to his flock, "as though he should never be old," and the same poor country-lad, crimped, kidnapped, brought into town, made drunk at an alehouse, turned into a wretched drummer-boy, with his hair sticking on end with powder and pomatum, a long cue at his back, and tricked out in the loathsome finery of the profession of blood:'

'He really was quite radical, wasn't he? I wonder if that last bit was influenced by his experience of being in the army?'

'Quite possibly. He was radical though like so many, I believe he changed his views somewhat as he became older. You have to remember, also, that there was a lot of poverty in Somerset at the time – and of course, the French Revolution had only recently occurred.'

I descended the pulpit.

'In essence,' she continued, 'Coleridge was always wedded in some way to religion and the church.'

'Can I have a look upstairs?'

'Yes, we can do a circuit.'

We ascended the stairs near the front of the church and to the upstairs pews.

We were now close to an imposing brass chandelier. I was almost close enough to reach out and touch it.

'That's impressive,' I said.

'It was donated by Taunton MP Nathaniel Webb in the early 1700s. The other notable thing about him was that he sat in the House of Commons for seven years and never once made a speech.'

'Not like Coleridge then.'

'No. I don't think Coleridge was ever short of words.'

'So that chandelier would have been here when Coleridge preached.'

'Yes.'

'I see it still holds candles.'

'Yes, we light it once a year at Christmas when we have our carol service.'

'How wonderful. Is there anything else I should know?'

'Well, just to put the Unitarian case for a moment. I think what we would like everyone to know is that we place particular emphasis on education and free thinking. We were the first in the town to give the opportunity of free education to girls as well as boys. The building next door was a school paid for by the Reverend Odgers. It was a great school in its day. Now it's a charity for the homeless. Another member of the chapel who was also a trustee and lay preacher was Dr. Malachi Blake. He founded the first hospital here.'

'Well thank you showing me around.'

'It's been a pleasure. But there is one other thing that you may be interested in while we're up here.'

She walked up to the pews at the back.

'Look,' she said and pointed to some carvings. 'The choir boys and the boys who pumped the organ used to sit up here and some of them left their mark.'

There were numerous inscriptions of names on the pews. One that stood out for me read V.G. Bond, Xmas 1902.

'I wonder if he fought in the war?' said Denise.

'Yes, I suppose he would be exactly the right age to be called up.'

There was also an inscription by S Poole, which made me wonder if that boy was related to Thomas Poole, Coleridge's good friend in Nether Stowey.

My phone bleeped at me. I had set the timer to remind me

to move on to the museum.

'I'd better go. I'm hoping to get the bus to Nether Stowey and have a quick trip to the museum before I go. Oh, and please can I give you something for your time.'

'If you would like to make a donation to the church that would be very welcome.'

We went downstairs and I made my donation. Denise accompanied me to the door.

'I know you don't have a lot of time, but, before you go for your bus, you may like to make a brief detour to the Temple Methodist Church just further up the street. It may be of particular interest to you as it was built by a bookseller.'

'Really!'

'Yes, and a very successful one. His name was James Lackington. His story is quite a fascinating one.'

I turned left out of the chapel, crossed the road and did as Denise suggested and walked up to the front of the Temple Methodist Church. The door was open. I walked in to see a community gathering where teas and coffees were being served. A bright and cheerful lady rescued me as I hesitated on the threshold. I explained briefly my interest, and she led me into the main part of the church, confirming the story about James Lackington that I had just heard from Denise.

'He was the son of a drunken shoemaker and did not have an easy start in life,' she explained, 'but he became apprenticed to another shoemaker in Taunton and eventually became a master shoemaker. Then he moved to London and set up a shop where he also began to sell books, which had always been a great love of his. The bookselling side of his business became so successful that he was able to move to an enormous shop in Finsbury Square which he called The Temple of the Muses. The shop was so large that it was said that you could drive a coach and horses around the inside of it.'

'Wow, we have trouble managing to get a buggy around our bookshop.'

'But he'd not forgotten about Taunton and his religious connections. He built the church in Taunton and sold it to a local Methodist group. The name that he had given to his bookshop became the name of the church today: The Temple.'

'How fascinating, and all as a result of his bookselling.'

Then someone shouted across, 'Joanna, have you got a minute?'

'Must dash, always busy – but you are welcome to stay as long as you want.'

I did not, in fact, stay much longer - though it was long enough to appreciate the majesty of space. There was upstairs seating as well. I wondered if all those spaces were ever filled.

The museum was only a short walk away and not too far from the bus stop. It boasted 400 million years of history. I thought of my friend Cameron. Faced with that, if he ever visited, he may never surface again. For myself, I only had time for a quick visit so I would be in time to take the early bus.

During the English Civil War, while much of the surrounding area was in Royalist hands, Taunton had supported Cromwell. In The Siege of Taunton, Cromwellian forces held out for two years before succumbing to Royalist forces. Admiral Blake, who led the defence of Taunton was famous for saying, 'I have four pairs of boots and would eat three pairs before I would surrender.'

Taunton had also witnessed the Duke of Monmouth declare himself King of England outside what was now the site of Marks and Spencer. Monmouth was the illegitimate son of Charles II and had led a rebellion against James II, from The Netherlands where he had gone into exile. He landed at Lyme Regis in June 1685 and marched towards Taunton picking up supporters along the way. Following a series of skirmishes, on 6 July 1685, there was the battle at Sedgemoor. It was a disaster for him. Monmouth and his rebels were routed by the King's army. Monmouth, himself, fled and was eventually discovered and executed. In what became known as the Bloody Assize, Judge Jeffreys, sentenced three hundred of the rebels to be hung, drawn and quartered and another nine hundred were transported to the West Indies to work on the sugar plantations.

There was also much more ancient history: a 200-million-year-old Plesiosaur fossil, the Low Ham Mosaic, the Frome Hoard and a stunning Cheddar Brooch. But I needed to move on to catch my bus.

9

After a meander through the town, the bus took the road north to the village of Kingston St Mary. On passing the Swan Inn, the road veered suddenly to the right before a sharp incline. It was very narrow at this point. A car mounted the verge towards the hedge to enable the bus to squeeze its way through. There was an exchange of smiles, a wave and flashing lights as we continued on our way.

Shortly after, a magnificent landscape unfolded of rolling hills dotted with cows and sheep. Then, after a few more minutes, the bus struggled in low gear as we approached the top of an impossibly steep hill. At a junction, there were roads to the right and left and a narrow road straight ahead. That was the one we took. There was a long descent followed by more twists and turns as we followed a fast-flowing stream. We passed Merridge Village Hall, and I saw a sign for Spaxton, the place my mother had mentioned. There were more tiny roads winding first one way and then the other until, eventually, the driver pulled up outside the old clock tower in Nether Stowey.

I spent a few moments getting my bearings before making my way along Lime Street. Ahead, in the distance, I saw the sign for the Ancient Mariner pub, named after perhaps Coleridge's best-known poem. Opposite the pub, I knew, was Coleridge Cottage.

A friendly and knowledgeable guide described in some detail the life at the cottage. Over the years it had been extended but in Coleridge's time it consisted of only two rooms at the front with three bedrooms upstairs. The kitchen immediately behind that looked quite spacious but was originally no more than a lean-to. Cooking was in the open fire in one of the rooms. If an oven was required, Sarah, Coleridge's wife, would take the food to the baker down the road to have it cooked. There was straw on the floor in Coleridge's day, and they were often plagued by mice. And yet, despite all the deprivations and many ups and downs, this had been a happy and productive time for Coleridge for much of the time that he was here.

Upstairs was a vivid portrait of Coleridge and an explanation of how he and Wordsworth had revolutionised literature and wrote poetry based on 'the real language of men' (presumably this included women, especially as Wordsworth's sister, Dorothy was such an important influence) and 'the spontaneous overflow of powerful feelings' rather than the more formal literature that preceded it.

In another of the upstairs rooms in one of the cabinets was displayed the sword Coleridge had worn when he joined the Dragoons. There was also a poem written in praise of Coleridge by Thomas Poole and a picture of Coleridge together with his brothers, James and George. George was, by all accounts, the perfect brother who often acted more like a father to Samuel, replacing the father he had lost when he was only eight. Another picture showed the room where he had lodged in Highgate with Dr Gilman later in life. The most impressive object to me was Coleridge's ornate writing desk and ink stand.

It was a bright sunny day, warm enough, when I had finished looking around the house, to sit out in the garden. I ordered tea and a scone and imagined Coleridge disappearing through the hedge at the bottom of the garden and seeking out his friend Thomas Poole in the house nearby. Poole was remarkable in his steadfastness and friendship of both Samuel and Sarah. His radical stance, though, was not welcomed by much of the local community. I reflected that Coleridge's friendship and support for him must have been very important to Poole too.

There were a series of poetry stations around the garden where you could listen to snippets of poetry by Coleridge and descriptions of Coleridge and the family. I heard "The Nightingale: A Conversation Poem" at the bottom of the garden while I drank my tea and ate my scone and, at the top of the garden, on a seat beneath a trimmed tree, a reading of "The Lime Tree Bower My Prison". This poem is extraordinary in its conception. At the time of the writing of the poem in July 1797, the Coleridge household had been joined by the Wordsworths from Racedown and Charles Lamb. Unfortunately, near the beginning of the visit from the Wordsworths and Lamb, Sarah spilt boiling milk over Coleridge's foot. He was burnt so badly that he was unable to accompany the rest of his friends on a walk into the Quantocks. It was a great disappointment to him, but he consoled himself by writing the poem.

What begins as a poem about anxiety and disappointment develops into an appreciation of his unexpected joy while being left behind and forced to remain sitting in the garden. He is able to empathise with his friend Charles Lamb (who has had a miserable time in the months leading up to his visit) and feels his own pleasure that his friend is experiencing the joys and benefits of walking in the Quantocks.

After I had listened to the poems, I thanked the guide and retraced my steps to the clock tower. I turned right into Castle Street. Leaving the village, I came to a cottage and an area known as Broomsquires, named after those who made brooms for a living. I then began the first of many steep ascents over the following days.

10

I took off my jacket before I crossed a field and started walking up another steep hill passing, as my instructions told me, near to a quarry which was the site of the Doddington copper mines in the 18th and early 19th century.

I thought I was alone, then all at once, as if out of nowhere three young people, a man and two women, came into my space, laughing and giggling. At first, I thought they were drunk as they were gambolling around, walking haphazardly and shouting excitedly.

I attempted to give them a decent berth, but they actually came straight towards me staring at what I guessed were their phones.

'Sorry,' one of them said. 'We're just trying to get a good signal we're not trying to attack you.'

'You can try my phone if you like,' another was saying.

'It's for the poetry.'

Then I remembered.

'Yes, I *do* know. The Quantock Poetry Trail. It's an app. I've already downloaded it.'

'Yes, I can hear it now,' a further one of them said.

I reached for my own phone and found the headphone symbol for the app. It made a boinging sound but nothing else happened. It was asking me to scan something.

'You need to scan a QR code the first time – to put the poem into the library on the app. I've got it here.'

One of the young women pulled out a piece of paper with a code on it. I scanned it and a map appeared and a pink blob.

'Thank you...'

'Arvinda... and that's Louisa and Kyle.'

'Nice to meet you.'

We all shook hands. I joined them as we all made our way towards the pink blob. All at once a poem appeared.

What's that swinging
in the creaking wind
over where the trees break?
Is it your conscience,
pecked by crows,
the old story,

or the devil himself, watching
between puzzled beeches
in an idle moment,

whistling his songs like wind
under the cottage door,
and seeping into your sleep?

It's nothing (some thought)
look away. He was good,
loved by all (they said)
and still more handsome
(they seem to remember)
after rotting there
a twelvemonth,
than anyone else in the village.

'Ah, a poem about John Walford,' said Louisa.

'Do you know the story?' asked Kyle.

'Only a little,' I said.

'Well, John Walford was a charcoal burner, and, as described in the poem, he was hanged for the murder of his wife, Jane Shorney – obviously, that was her maiden name,' he continued. 'He'd been engaged to Ann Rice, but the marriage was cancelled, it is said because of his mother taking against Ann. Then he got Jane pregnant, and they were married.'

'This is close to where it all happened, isn't it?' said Louisa.

'Yes, they had only been married three weeks when she went off to the local pub, The Castle of Comfort, one Saturday night, not far from here,' continued Kyle. 'Walford followed her. Apparently, he'd planned to leave her and go to London, but his plans had been frustrated and, the story goes, this had been playing on his mind, and it turned into rage. He hit out at her and then beat her unconscious with a post from the hedge and fractured her skull. Then he cut her throat and returned to his house.'

'As you can hear from the poem,' said Arvinda, 'there was a lot of sympathy for him and they talked about how handsome he was and how Jane was a simpleton.'

We continued walking up the hill. Another poem jumped out at us entitled "The View from Walford's Gibbet", describing the view across to Hinckley Point, which we could clearly see in the distance. The poem describes how *Their gibbets be almost 10 times higher an mine! and laments how it represents umanity? Decayed.*

Though they were a chatty group, they all listened in respectful silence to the poem.

'That's really good,' Louisa said. 'What a great idea.'

'Are you walking far?' asked Arvinda.

'I'm doing the Coleridge Way.'

'That's a good walk,' she said.

'Over a few days. I'm hoping to get to Roadwater today. Well, not hoping, I have to. I have a bed and breakfast booked there.'

'We'll walk a little of the way with you if you don't mind some company,' said Kyle.

'As long as we don't hold you up,' said Louisa.

'No, it would be good to have some company.'

'And the exercise will do us some good,' said Arvinda.

They asked what I did and were impressed by the fact that I owned a bookshop.

'It must be so cool having your own bookshop,' said Kyle.

'How do you ever get any work done? Don't you just feel like reading books all day?' said Louisa.

'That would be nice but, the truth is, I just don't have time to read books at work. There's just too much to do.'

They were all poets who had published their own work and one of them had recently won a prize. I offered to stock their books in my bookshop if they sent me some copies. They said that they hoped to visit my bookshop someday.

They were good company. I told them about my visit to the

Coleridge Society and said I was going to attend the open day, but did not mention that I would be presenting *Lyrical Ballads* to them.

They knew quite a bit about Coleridge, about The Rime of the "Ancient Mariner" and "Kubla Kahn" of course, but also about "Christabel" and particularly "Frost at Midnight" which they recommended as a particularly fine poem.

Arvinda recited the first two lines

The Frost performs its secret ministry,
Unhelped by any wind. The owlet's cry...

'Have you read it?'she asked me.

'I think I have heard it read at a talk on Coleridge once, but I'm not sure if I can claim to know it.'

'I'll tell you anyway. It's all about his loneliness as a child at Christ's Hospital and how he was deprived of nature, and he hopes that his newborn son will not have the same experience and have a life connected to nature.'

'I love the last lines,' said Louisa, '*the secret ministry of frost shall hang them up in silent icicles, quietly shining to the quiet moon. I just think that's brilliant.'*

'Do you give poetry readings?' I asked.

'Yes, no use writing poetry if you don't read it,' said Kyle.

'We have a local poetry group,' I said. 'Some of them are very good and have published their own work, like you. They meet in our bookshop every few months and are very keen to hear guest poets. If you want to, I can put them in touch with you.'

'That would be great.'

'Have you always written poetry?' I said to Arvinda.

'Not exactly. My mum always loved poetry – which I could not understand. It put me right off it. Then I met this boy who loved poetry, which I found even more bizarre. But he was patient with me, explained what he thought was good, took me to some poetry readings – and then wrote a poem about me. And then I was hooked!'

'Who was this amazing boy?'

She put her arm around Kyle.

'Then I just had to marry him.'

'Oh, amazing. What a great story.'

'It wasn't that great a poem, but it gave me what I wanted,' said Kyle wryly.

We all laughed.

'I think we should give my mum the credit really,' said Arvinda. 'You know she was of that generation. She was really clever but didn't have the opportunity to go to university. But that didn't stop her. She learnt about poetry all by herself. She actually produced a volume of poetry which I now keep by my bed.'

I could not then help relating the story of my mother and her university course and her impending visit to the West Country.

At this point the party left me to visit Dowsborough Iron Age Fort, which was off the main route of the walk. Much as I would have liked to accompany them, I had a good walk ahead of me and was already behind schedule. We said our goodbyes, and they made promises to visit my bookshop.

Before I began my journey to Somerset, I had looked up Alfoxden, the home that the Wordsworths lived in for a year. I discovered that, while it had once become a hotel, it had been sadly neglected in recent years and had lain empty for some time. It had, though, perhaps an unlikely recent saviour when it was bought by the Triratna Buddhist Community, an international fellowship of Buddhists with a westward slant. Part of their mission, apart from running retreats and other events, was to restore the house and honour its position as the home of one of our greatest poets.

My first thought as I approached the house, with its white rendered frontage, was how grand it was in comparison with Coleridge's cottage in Lime Street. The Coleridges themselves were originally to have a more substantial residence at Adscombe, a pretty hamlet near Over Stowey, but the arrangement had fallen through. Thomas Poole had become a firm friend when Coleridge had visited Nether Stowey in 1794 in the company of Robert Southey, although Poole was much more impressed by Coleridge than by Southey. Poole had secured a small cottage called Gilbard's at the top of Lime Street in Nether Stowey as 'a last resort', but so desperate was Coleridge to leave Clevedon following his marriage 'to live in a beautiful country' and be near Poole that he went along with it.

Wordsworth appeared to be luckier than his friend in general when finding accommodation. He had previously been found a house with his sister at Racedown, near Yeovil, for which he paid no rent, even though it was fully furnished and where they began fostering a three-year-old boy called Basil Montague. It was to this house that Coleridge had embarked on a 40 mile walk from Nether Stowey to meet Wordsworth and Dorothy. They all got on so well that Coleridge persuaded Wordsworth and Dorothy to move nearer to him in Somerset. While the Wordsworths were on a walk following a visit to Coleridge, they spotted Alfoxden House and, on making enquiries, found that it was for rent. It seemed, once again, that fortune was on their side.

The house did not appear to be open but there was no one stopping me from exploring the grounds. Behind the house was a beautiful ancient oak tree, known as the Domesday Oak as it was believed to date back to that period. I sat down for a moment and took a drink from my flask. While I sat, I marvelled at the bulbous trunk and the limbs of thick branches extending upwards and outwards. I liked the thought that Wordsworth and Coleridge would have sat by this very same tree, perhaps in the very same spot I was sitting.

The walk between Nether Stowey and Alfoxden was one that Coleridge and the Wordsworths regularly took. Part of me did wonder whether the Wordsworths and the Coleridges could have joined forces, and all moved into Alfoxden. In that case, though, Coleridge would have lost the easy access to Tom Poole and his extensive library.

I returned to the path and continued on my way at a good pace. There were delightful streams to cross (which I managed without getting my feet wet), some footbridges and then open moorland and rolling green pastureland followed by a woodland path. A further steep climb was rewarded with a view across the valley to Exmoor and the coast. Then I descended into the pretty village of Bicknoller. There was a pub. I was roughly half-way along my walk for the day.

Time, I thought, for a late lunch, if they had not stopped serving, as it was now well after 2.30 pm.

I was in luck, as a Cornish pasty was on offer. I decided I could afford to treat myself to a 15 minute stop. The pasty was accompanied by a pint of best bitter. I sat in the outside garden besides a boules court.

'Didn't think I would find boules in Somerset,' I said to a couple who were sitting on the adjacent bench.

'Ah, that's to do with the nuclear power station at Hinckley,' said the man. 'All the French there, see. But you know, we all join in. We like it. It makes a change from skittles.'

I wondered what Wordsworth and Coleridge would have thought of the nuclear power station.

'Are you from these parts?' his partner asked.

I explained about my walk.

'You'll do well to get to The Valiant Soldier tonight,' he said.'I think you'll enjoy it there, though. It's a pretty spot at Roadwater,'

The pasty was delicious as was the beer. I felt in the mood for another but was already feeling a little sleepy, as well as being conscious about the time. I needed to walk it off and wake myself up, so I resisted the temptation and went on my way.

Soon after leaving the village, I crossed the main road, the first time I had encountered anything but a minor road since the beginning of the walk. I waited for a convoy of vehicles to pass. I was pleased to leave the road behind and once more return to fields and hedges. I felt happy and a little elated. This walk was beginning to do me good.

Another significant barrier to my route occurred shortly after in the form of a railway line. It was the route of the West Somerset Railway, the longest private steam railway in the country (I had read). It was a shame, I thought, that I did not have the opportunity of travelling on it.

I was looking forward to the fact that Esther would be driving down to walk with me the following day. She was going to make an early start and meet me at The Valiant Soldier for breakfast. We would walk together for one day, staying one night at Porlock before she took an early morning bus back to Minehead and then make a short walk to pick up her car.

I had hoped she could accompany me for longer, but she wanted to keep her stay to a minimum so that Aggie was not left for too long on her own. Our student was only available some of the time as it coincided with her holiday.

There were further quiet country roads and fields until I reached the village of Sampford Brett. From there, a steady climb was followed by an ancient green lane and a footpath across a field until I reached Monksilver and another attractive-looking pub, The Knotley Arms. I glanced at the enticing menu and took a moment to read about the origins of Monksilver. It was not known by that name until the fourteenth century and was mentioned in the Domesday Book as 'Selvre'. The origins of the silver part of the name were either the Latin 'silva' for wood or the Saxon 'sulfhere', a description of the silvery stream which runs through the village. I liked to think it was the latter.

After another steep climb out of the village, I followed a sign to Carlton Cross accompanied by a brook. And then I was once more on an upward trajectory to Bird's Hill where I entered an extensive area of woodland. I carefully followed the blue marks on the trees as there were a variety of paths to the left and right, until I reached open heathland. At Carlton Cross I crossed a road as instructed by my guide. I was then told to ignore the permitted path to the viewpoint on the right. This time, though, I went against the instructions and climbed the small hillock where I was rewarded with a breathtaking view.

I took a few photos and returned to the route until, after a short while, I crossed a field and took a path down the north side of Beacon Hill. There was another main road and a short walk steeply downhill before I crossed a road that led onto a track by Chidgley Hill Farm. I was now on the Roadwater Valley route following a line of beech trees on top of a high bank. I entered Pitt Wood and carried on past a sign to The Old Mineral Line, which, I had read, transported iron ore to Watchet on the coast where it was shipped to the steel works at Ebbw Vale across the water in Wales. More open ground gave way to woodland. I crossed a bridge by a pretty thatched cottage and then began following the lane into the village as there were the first signs of the softening of the suns rays and approaching twilight.

I passed a community post office and a village hall, but my destination was, I knew, on the edge of the village. I continued walking and shortly after found on my right The Valiant Soldier where I had booked a room for the night. I had made up good time covering my 19 miles, following a late start, and felt the need of a good meal, a pint of beer and a good night's sleep.

11

Before I went into the pub I took a photo of the distinctive pub sign, which appeared to be hewn out of metal. It depicted a soldier in a blue and black striped vestment and a black helmet, brandishing a curved sabre above his head in preparation to strike a blow.

'I'll show you to your room,' said the man behind the bar.

'That's an interesting sign you have there,' I said as we ascended the stairs towards my room.

'Ah, that's by Rachel Reckitt. She was a local artist. The family lived in a beautiful house at Golsoncott not far from here. I think they open the gardens sometimes in the summer. Beautiful they are, too.'

He opened the door.

'All right for you?' he said.

'Yes, perfect. I spoke to someone about leaving my friend's car here for a day. She is joining me at breakfast tomorrow. Just wanted to check that's still OK.'

'Yes, it was me you spoke to. That's fine. We'll keep an eye on it for her.'

Though I was hot and a little sweaty, I decided that I would shower later, afraid that I would miss out on an evening meal. I deposited my rucksack and went back down to the bar.

I should ring Esther to check that everything is OK for her trip tomorrow, I thought. I ordered some food and sat myself down at a table near the bar. When I found Esther's number, I saw that she had tried me three times in the last two hours. I checked my settings and saw that my phone had been switched to silent.

She answered immediately, when I rang.

'Where were you? I was getting worried about you.'

'Sorry, I somehow managed to switch my phone to silent.'

'Listen, I have a problem with my car. It died on me yesterday and it will take a couple of days to fix.'

I was crestfallen. I had been looking forward to her visit.

'Why don't you use my car. You have a key to my house. I think the keys are hanging up in the usual place.'

'You would have to put me on your insurance,' she said. 'It might be a bit fiddly.'

'So, does that mean you're not coming?'

'Don't worry, I have a solution. I'm coming to see you on Aggie's Lambretta!'

'What? Do you even know how to ride one?'

'Of course, I had a scooter when I was younger. Anyway, I'm all set for tomorrow. I plan to be there by eight.'

'Great! But be careful. Have you got a helmet?'

'I'm borrowing Aggie's.'

'But...'

'But what?'

'Well, Aggie's got quite a small head.'

'And you think I've got a big head. You know how to charm a girl. In fact, it fits perfectly.'

We talked briefly about the bookshop and my walk so far. I gave her some brief instructions about finding the pub.

My fish pie arrived. I was pleased to see that they had Cask Marque certification for the keeping of real ales and selected a local Exmoor Ale to accompany the meal. I went for their 3.8% classic bitter. I had in mind the fact that Esther had promised to arrive early in the morning and did not want to overdo it by drinking strong beer.

I had not appreciated how hungry the walk had made me and within a few minutes had all but finished my meal. As I was contemplating my shower and an early bedtime, a stream of people rushed in. Until then, I had been the only person sitting and eating in the pub bar. The recent influx all seemed to know each other and were ordering drinks in a hurry. One of them was talking loudly on the phone.

'All right, if you can't you can't,' I heard him say to someone at the other end of his phone. He turned to one of his friends. 'That's it, Bill definitely can't come. The jobs too important, he says.'

'What can be more important than skittles?'

There was general laughter, but I could see the concern on his face.

49

'I don't suppose someone can play twice, for our side.'

'It's not really fair though, is it?'

'I suppose not.'

'Sorry, Nathan, I'm the only one on,' said the barman. 'Sally will be coming later but not until half-nine.'

That was the man serving behind the bar, apologising I guessed, for not being able to play.

'No, that's too late.'

He gave a glance towards me.

'We can at least have a drink.'

'Yeah.'

He looked at me again and this time smiled. I smiled back.

'I don't suppose you could step in?'

It took me a while to realise that he was speaking to me.

'Step in?'

'We have a skittles match, but we're one short.'

'I've never played.'

'The rules are easy,' the man next to him said.

'I've played ten pin bowling.'

'There you are then. It's not so very different. Only better,' continued the man.

'We'll cover your match fees,' said the man who I now knew was called Nathan.

'And buy you a drink,' said the other man.

'Or two,' said another.

I wanted to say no, tell them that I needed my shower and bed but did not find the words. Instead, I said:

'All right, if you can give me a few minutes explaining the rules.'

'That we can,' said Nathan. 'Sorry, I didn't get your name?'

'Elliot.'

'Step inside, Elliot.'

He gestured towards the door of the skittle alley.

'There is one problem, though,' his mate said.

'What's that?'

'We need to know: do you drink cider or beer?'

They all laughed

As I had been drinking beer, I decided to stick with it, and another pint was pulled for me.

'This way.'

I followed them through the doorway into an impressive looking skittle alley, all set up and ready to go. It had access and viewing areas all down one side and an impressive looking scoreboard headed Valiant Soldier Skittles.

I felt a sudden moment of trepidation and nerves at my own inexperience.

'You'll be on our team, The Night Riders.'

'The basic idea couldn't be simpler,' Nathan said. 'You throw this wooden ball underarm at those nine wooden skittles down the alley. You get to throw the ball three times per go. If after the first or second go you have knocked down all nine skittles, then all nine will be stood up again for you to have another go at. In theory you can get a maximum score per go of 27, but because of the spacing of the skittles this is virtually impossible to achieve.'

'Not for some of us,' said one of his friends puffing his chest out.

'That was just luck last week. I don't expect we'll ever see that again in our lifetime. Anyway, as I was explaining, knocking down all nine skittles with two throws is called a spare. Getting spares is what really separates the good skittler from the average skittler – but just do what you can. If you go last, you can get the hang of it by seeing what the others do. Your score is the total number of skittles you knock over.'

'I'll try and remember that.'

I think he could see the concern on my face.

'It's just a bit of fun really.'

A bit of fun it may have been but as soon as the play started, I could see an intensity and concentration in the faces of all of those playing the game that suggested otherwise. When it came to my turn I felt a flutter in my stomach. If I had been of a religious frame of mind, I may have crossed myself as I stepped up to the line.

I was given last minute instructions, including a special mention about not crossing that line.

Thankfully, my first throw kept to the middle and did not disappear down the side. Though I was pleased to see it roll straight down the middle, I was not so pleased that I only knocked down one of the skittles.

'Good start,' said one of them encouragingly.

Nathan, though, whispered in my ear.

'A little too straight. See if you can do it a little off centre next time.'

I tried as he said and was rewarded with a further three skittles tumbling to the floor.

'Bit of beginners luck there,' said another, so I knew I was not making a real hash of it.

I was secretly pleased with myself but, at the same time, I envied the next thrower who managed to knock all but one down and then proceeded to knock the single remaining one down with the next throw.

'He's only got a spare!' I heard someone cry.

'How long does it last?' I asked.

'We play five legs – so you get five goes.'

As we went through the successive legs, my interest became aroused. There were obviously a couple of key players that racked up high scores on either side and each time they came on to throw they were cheered enthusiastically. We were only slightly behind as we came to the last round with me going last so that an average throw from me should be enough for us to win. However, my nerves got to me and my first throw went down the side of the alley for the first time that evening. There was some talk about letting me off as a beginner and it even had some support of the players on the other side, though one or two protested that it would not be fair as it was a league game. Until that moment I had no idea that it was. I put up my hand.

'No, I don't want any favours,' I said heroically.

I rolled my second ball with some force with my eyes half-closed and turned my back. There was a roar from one of my teammates. I looked round to see that I had knocked down six skittles, my best score of the night.

We all shook hands. More pints were bought on all sides. I had not bought a single drink all night so grateful were they that I had filled in for the absent player. I was now onto my fourth pint and was being urged to have a fifth.

I had to be persistent in my refusal. I explained that I had an early start and was eventually allowed to make my way to bed accompanied by slaps on my back.

'You should do it more regular,' said one. 'You have the makings of a good player.'

It was now eleven-thirty, much later than I had intended going to bed, and I needed a shower. I was also a little drunk, aided by the fact that they had switched my pints from the moderate alcohol content of the classic bitter to a strong bitter which was 4.8%. I was told it would put hair on my chest. I was not sure that I wanted any more hair on my chest but felt I did not have much say in the matter. I was in bed by twelve but found trouble sleeping. I kept running over in my head the excitement of the skittles game and my part in it.

12

When the alarm on my watch went off at 7 am the following morning, I felt as though I had only just gone to sleep. I did not have a headache from the beer that I had drunk the previous night, but my head was fuzzy, and I felt dozy. If it were not for the fact that Esther was arriving, I would have turned over and set the alarm for another hour.

I was in the bar area for my breakfast by 7.30. I had also packed my rucksack ready for a quick departure and had my key ready for checking out. I selected the full English breakfast, a tried and tested way of restoring myself the morning after a beer-drinking session.

The man serving was the same person who was on the bar the previous night. I found out that he was in fact the landlord.

'Seems like you do everything around here,' I said to him.

'Feels like that sometimes,' he said, 'but I'm going to get a break and a game of golf this afternoon.'

We commiserated with each other for a moment over the responsibilities of running our mutual businesses. Afterwards he reflected on the previous evening.

'That was a good session last night by all accounts. I think you made yourself popular by stepping in for the skittles.'

'Well, I enjoyed it,' I said truthfully. 'Though I was a bit nervous to begin with.'

'They do love their skittles round here. Whereabouts you off today then?'

'Porlock.'

'That's a decent walk.'

'14 miles according to my guide.'

'I think you'll like Porlock. And you have somewhere to stay?'

'Yes, The Ship Inn.'

'You'll be all right there. They run a decent place, by all accounts.'

'Oh, and there's a change of plan. My friend, she's now coming by scooter rather than by car.'

'Your girlfriend. Yes, that's no problem. If she just leaves it at the corner of the car park, I'll keep an eye on it for her.'

I did not bother correcting him about calling Esther my girlfriend.

'Will she want breakfast before she sets off?'

'She might,' I said. 'I'll ask her.'

I should have asked her the night before. We could have had breakfast together. I didn't want to ring her while she was riding. I continued with my own order.

Orange juice, bacon, eggs, sausages, tomatoes, mushrooms and, I was delighted to see, black pudding, plus a pot of tea and I felt myself reviving. I was on my third cup of tea and was topping off my breakfast with a slice of toast and marmalade, made by the local WI, when I heard the distinctive sound of Aggie's Lambretta. I went outside to meet Esther.

Esther already had her helmet off and neatly tucked under her arm by the time I caught up with her. She gave me a brief hug and agreed to a cup of tea and a piece of toast. As previously arranged, she had brought something for our lunch. The sun was beginning to peep through the clouds. We decided to sit at one of the tables outside.

'How's the shop?' I asked.

'Much as you left it. You've only been away for a day and a bit. Were you expecting it to collapse without your presence?'

'It seems longer than a day and a half. I seem to have done so much already.'

I explained more about my walk and the fantastic variety of landscape and my encounter with the poetry group. Then I told her about the skittles.

'That's so typical of you. I thought you were looking a bit sleepy.'

'I've also walked 19 miles, well 18 and three-quarters, according to the guide.'

I wheeled her Lambretta round to the yard as instructed by the landlord while Esther organised her toast and tea. By the time I had finished my ablutions and checked out, Esther was ready to go.

We turned right out of the pub and continued along the narrow road. We passed a fishery and then left the road and made a long climb on a path through Langridge Wood.

'That's a challenging start to the day,' said Esther when we finally reached what appeared to be the top of the hill and the ground began to flatten out.

'It's always the same,' I said. 'Just about every new stretch seems to start with the words "a steep ascent".'

Soon after, though, we began what felt like a perilous descent along a rocky path towards Luxborough. It was the kind of path where it was so steep that it was difficult to walk without running and made your calf muscles ache. There was another nice-looking pub when we reached Luxborough, The Royal Oak, and a pretty collection of houses - but our route was in the opposite direction, and it was not long before we were climbing once more. Up and up we went to the top of Colly Hill and emerged from some trees into a glorious view across the valley. We sat down and took our first rest.

Esther laid back using her rucksack as a pillow.

'This is brilliant. So glad I came.'

She looked across to me.

'We should do more of this Elliot.'

'Yes, we should.'

Five minutes later we continued on our upward path, this time up Lype Hill, a broad swathe of green which I noticed on the map had a spot height of 421 metres. It felt at that moment as though we were on top of the world. We were passed by two women on horseback who confirmed that we were going in the right direction to Cutcombe, our next destination. Shortly after, we crossed a road that led to a private hotel and then continued down a green lane until it became a rough stone path. The route guide warned that it can be slippery when wet, but it was mercifully dry.

We then reached Cutcombe Cross and headed for signs towards Dunkery Beacon, the highest point in Somerset at over 1700 feet. Our plan, though, was to bypass the beacon and we headed for the hamlet of Brockwell. We descended into woods and at a fork marked Tom's Path took the upward track.

'Wow, this is amazing,' said Esther.

The path was steep and wound its way through a variety of trees growing out from impossibly steep banks. The temperature had risen quickly that morning and it was refreshingly cool underneath the leafy canopy. Eventually we descended to a stream and found a perfect place for a late lunch.

'We're doing quite well. We can afford a bit of a rest,' I said.

'Good. I'll sort the lunch out.'

Esther proceeded to unload her rucksack. She took out a red and white tea towel which served as a tablecloth, and began to unload the contents of her rucksack. There were crusty baguettes, Parma ham, salami, St Agur cheese, a green salad, tomatoes, grapes and apples.

'This isn't just a meal it's a veritable feast,' I said.

She smiled.

'I do my best, though I haven't finished yet.'

She reached back into the rucksack and took out a bottle of wine and two wine glasses.

'Oh, that's just perfect. But I'm not sure you can afford it on your salary.'

'I didn't have to. Simon turned up at the shop and heard that I was coming down to see you. A few minutes later he returned with a bottle. It's a Pinot Noir. He said we would not want something too heavy if we were having it with our lunch.'

I looked at the label and read Domaine Camus Bruchon Savigny-Lès-Beaune Cuvée Reine Jol. Not something I had ever seen at the local supermarket.

'I love how he always gets his priorities right. And you've got real wine glasses!'

Esther knew how important this was to me.

'I'm afraid I only have paper plates.'

'That's OK. I'll slum it.'

We tucked into our food.

'Something special about a picnic outside,' I said.

'Most picnics are outside.'

'OK, a picnic outside, next to a stream after a long walk.'

I wanted to add *with you* but did not.

'OK, yes I can agree with that.'

I made a salami, cheese and salad baguette out of the assembled offerings, nibbled on cheese and ate a whole tomato in one go.

'How about a glass of wine then?' suggested Esther.

'I don't suppose it's a screwtop?'

'It's OK.'

She pulled out a corkscrew attached to a penknife. Quite small, but a corkscrew nevertheless.

She began to screw into the cork. I was not sure the corkscrew was sufficient for the job.

'Are you sure that's gonna work?'

'Well, I know I should look for a big strong man to help me out…'

'But you can't find one…'

She deftly pulled out the cork with a satisfying pop and smiled.

'I can't find one and I don't need one, thank you very much.'

She splashed some wine into my glass and into her own. We clinked glasses.

'Cheers!' we both said.

It did not take us long to demolish the whole bottle.

'You know, the last time I remember doing something like this was when I was with Cameron on that bike ride in Kent.'

'I wondered how long it would be before you would invoke his name. It was his fault that you got involved in all that business in Italy in the first place.'

'That's a little unfair - if substantially true.'

Esther, though, had moved onto other things and was taking her walking shoes and socks off.

'That stream looks too enticing,' she said.

She tucked up her shorts (they were the long variety) as far as they would go and was off into the middle of the stream.

'Come on,' she said.

I followed her. The water was cooling and refreshing. I refrained from telling her I had also splashed through water with Cameron on another occasion similar to this. We walked up and down the stream and then collapsed onto the bank.

'The trouble with all that nice food and wine is it makes you a little bit sleepy,' I said. 'I wonder if we can afford a short nap. We're doing pretty well for time.'

'OK, a short one. I'll put 30 minutes on the alarm, no more.'
She lay down and then a moment later said:

'The trouble is I need a pillow.'

She lifted up her rucksack, placed it unceremoniously on my lap and lay her head down.

'I seem to remember you did something like this on a bench when we interviewed Grindley at the University. And I don't remember Cameron asking me if I could be his pillow.'

'Shush,' she said. 'We don't have much time.'

I did not sleep at first. I felt in state of perfect harmony as I listened to the stream bubbling along. And then at some point we must have both drifted off because the next thing I knew the alarm on Esther's phone was making its insistent noise and, rather comically, we both awoke with a start, screaming at each other.

We had our rucksacks re-packed in seconds. I was feeling a little bleary eyed and I guessed Esther was the same. There is nothing better, however, than a walk to get the circulation going and restore yourself to a state of wakefulness. We began climbing uphill again until we exited the woodland path we had been following and emerged onto open moorland called Dunkery Errish.

Whether it was our sleepiness after the lunch or not, for the first time that day we became confused about the way. The reassuring blue marks and the quill indicating the Coleridge way seemed to have disappeared. We were not sure whether to go forwards or to the right. Perhaps in our postprandial state we had missed a turning. The guide told us we should be heading north. Following Esther's compass on her phone we found a gate and a path leading steeply downhill which, however, did not have any way markings. We forded a river, all the time making sure we were heading north and in the direction of Brockwell. At last, we saw a reassuring sign with a quill on it indicating that we were going in the right direction.

Another steep descent took us to a small stream at Hanley Combe. From there we climbed until we were walking parallel to a hedge. We followed a rough track across heathland and to trees at Higher Brockwell. Then we were in a wooded area once more and following a bridleway before we took a left-hand path indicating the landmark of Webber's Post.

Here we found a busy car park, which we cut diagonally across. We were now once again in woodland and following a path to Chapel Cross. We passed a farm and a mill and then a delightful packhorse bridge where we took a few moments to stare at the gushing water below. We crossed a cattle grid marking the boundary, the sign said, of the Holnicote Estate and stumbled onto a mixture of roads and footpaths before eventually turning left along the delightfully named street of Drang to arrive at St Dubricius Church in the centre of Porlock. We were making good time despite getting a little lost earlier on, time enough for a rest in the churchyard on a characterful octagonal seat in the shade of a tree. Esther had one more culinary trick up her sleeve and produced a small flask of sweet coffee. It was still warm and reviving.

'You were telling me earlier about your extended essay.'

'Yes, well everybody seems to celebrate Coleridge's early genius and his thwarted ambitions, but they don't acknowledge the important role of Sarah or how she suffered and how her own ambitions were put on the back burner.'

'Do you mean her literary ambitions?'

'I don't mean like Dorothy. Her writings were extraordinary – just look at her journals – and may well have contributed to some of William's poems. But Sarah was intelligent and could write a good letter. I suppose I mean more that any ambitions she might have entertained were sacrificed by the fact that she was treated like a drudge and had to look after the children and survive in the most difficult of circumstances.'

'Perhaps they were just not the right people for each other.'

'That was what Coleridge would have you believe – that is what he said later – but I think that is just a cop-out. Whether it was true or not, he surely should have felt more responsibility and contributed more – and that business of going to the Haas Mountains and extending his stay even though he knew his child was seriously ill – leaving Sarah to shoulder the responsibility on her own – that was thoughtless and self-indulgent.'

'What about his opium addiction?'

'He did that to himself.'

'But didn't he originally take it for his bad leg or fever or something?'

'That's what he claimed and, it's true, opium in the form of laudanum was taken for all sorts of ailments at that time. But it was ultimately in his own hands.'

'Southey just thought he was being lazy and self-indulgent,' I said.

'Southey never forgave him for falling out with him for back-tracking on the Pantisocracy. Southey, though, started it by compromising and wanting servants which was totally against the democratic principles of the original Pantiscocracy. The women who were to accompany them were already being treated like second-class citizens in any case. He wrote Southey a brilliant very passionate letter. I have to admit I am on Coleridge's side there. Despite all his failings, he was very principled. Besides, going back to the accusation of laziness, Dr Gilman, the doctor who treated Coleridge for his opium addiction when he moved to Highgate, said all that stuff about his being lazy was nonsense.'

'So now you're justifying his behaviour whereas earlier you were criticising him for becoming addicted.'

'I never said that he wasn't a complex character but, whichever way you look at it and whatever the reasons, Sarah was badly treated. She had to survive in that tiny cottage...'

'Yes, I know I was there.'

'And rush down the road if they wanted anything baked – as they did not have a proper oven...'

'I know I have seen it... the kitchen, I mean...'

'And he was forever escaping next door to Tom Poole...'

'Yes, I have sat in the garden.'

She turned on me.

'Will you please stop agreeing with me! It's very unsettling.'

She rose from the seat and with one easy motion put her rucksack on her back and began walking. I ran after her, not wishing to be left behind.

We continued along the main road for a little way then headed up Porlock Hill before turning right onto a road which became the Woodland Toll Road. We skirted the edge of the woodland and then crossed a stream at Allerpark Combe. There was more woodland and another stream to cross, and a descent to a row of houses at West Porlock. After another steep climb we were rewarded briefly with a downhill walk to a stream at Hawknest Combe, though within minutes we were again walking in an upward direction through more trees above Porlock Weir. We could see the Weir beneath us, but our instructions told us to ignore the path downwards. However, for once we felt able to disobey the instructions as this was to be our destination for the night. We took the path down, though I thought, ruefully, that I would have to come back using the same steep path the next morning.

13

Shortly afterwards, we saw the enticing site of the 15th century Ship Inn, our accommodation for the night. Esther and I had agreed to save money by booking a twin room at the inn. I gave the landlord my booking details.

'Ah, now there is a slight bit of a problem,' he said. 'I didn't know if you could help me out. I was going to try and contact you but we have been so busy.'

'Is there something wrong?' I asked.

'We do have a room, sir, no problem with that. It's just we had a request from another couple, an older couple as you may say. Well, the thing is, he needs to be getting up in the night, has a few issues and she would like to get a proper night's sleep. I took the liberty of moving them last night into the only twin room available, well, not really available because it is your room by rights, but I said I would ask you, to see if you would not mind.'

'Into our room?'

'Yes, I'm sorry. I didn't know what else to do. I can give you a special rate.'

It was a *fait accompli* I had it in mind to say, but I also thought it was probably unreasonable for us to refuse and we had nowhere else to stay for the night. He looked at us. I could see he was sizing us up, wondering what on earth was wrong with us that we could not sleep together in a double bed.

'He snores,' said Esther. 'You've never heard anything like it. In fact, it's fair to warn you that he may wake up the whole hotel. I need my sleep too.'

He gave a hearty laugh.

'Well, I think I may have a solution, quite a good one too. If you were able to switch rooms, I could give you the top room in the hotel for the same price as the twin room. I could make you up a separate bed – it's a big room with plenty of space and we do this for families sometimes – obviously not as luxurious as the master bed but its more than a camp bed, quite comfortable in its way, though I don't think it would have done for the other gentleman. Then you can snore away in the corner…' he looked at me (was it with contempt or sympathy?) 'to your hearts content without disturbing your lady friend over-much.'

It was embarrassing and uncomfortable for me and I felt my face going red in the way I had not experienced since I was a teenager.

'That will do nicely,' said Esther, 'very nicely indeed.'

'I think you will like the room.'

He was now talking to Esther while I, the poor ignorant snorer, the source of the problem, stood timidly looking on. We signed our names and followed him to the accommodation.

The room was just as he had said with another bed in the corner away from the main bed, at the moment plied with cushions, obviously used as a substitute sofa when it was not in use as an extra bed.

'If I give you a few minutes to settle yourselves I will arrange for someone to make up the bed.'

'Yes, that's fine,' I said. 'We'll come down and order some food.'

I was attempting to impose myself on the situation.

'Right you are,' he said, but when he spoke, he looked at Esther rather than me as though seeking her approval.

'Look, Esther,' I said, when he had gone 'I'm not even sure if I do snore. The only time you heard me was when I had quite a lot to drink.'

The occasion had been after we had visited Aggie's house one day and I had forgotten I was driving. I had too much to drink and had walked back to Esther's house and stayed on her sofa for the night.

'Hmm. We'll see, shall we?'

It was still quite early, so we decided to spend a little time on the Weir.

We walked through the car park and crossed a footbridge towards the harbour and the Quay. There was a large seating area in the lea of the harbour wall, perfect for soaking up the sun or, I guessed, sheltering from the wind when the weather was not so good. We crossed through a gap, passing brightly coloured cottages, and onto the pebbly beach. The pebbles were large and irregular and uncomfortable to walk on, but the sea was inviting, and the sky was cloudless and warming. We made our way down to the sea edge and sat ourselves down. For the second time that day we removed our socks and put our feet in the water.

'Would be nice to have a swim,' I said.

'It's a bit pebbly and no towels. I think I am just happy cooling my feet in the water – but we must come for a day on the beach another time, If not here, somewhere else.'

'Perhaps somewhere with more sand.'

'Yes, that would be good.'

'This will do, for now.'

She put her hand on mine for the briefest of moments.

When we returned to the Inn, the landlord informed us that he had made the extra bed up in the room. We ordered our food, the fillet of wild bream for me, butter-nut squash and sage penne pasta with roasted Mediterranean vegetables for Esther.

Our food arrived. We ordered a bottle of Pinot Grigio to go with it.

'You are more like Cameron than you know. You just can't resist the good things in life where food and drink are concerned.'

'Well, I know I'm a poor substitute for Cameron, but I think we should drink his health anyway.'

'Ah, yes, well there's more than one reason to do that.'

I explained about his forthcoming book and possible series. I had not yet found an opportunity to relay on to her my conversation with him.

'That's great. We must have him down to do a talk at the shop.'

'Exactly my thought,' I said.

There were a few moments of companionable silence while we were both lost in our own thoughts. Esther went to the bathroom.

'You know, what occurs to me,' I said when she returned. 'It's called the Coleridge Way, but the Wordsworths did the walks as well.'

'I suppose it's because Coleridge had his roots in the West Country. And he was here for a bit longer. But I see your point.'

'In fact, we've not talked much about Wordsworth.'

'You mean the Wordsworths.'

'I suppose I do.'

'Dorothy was a big influence – both in her effect on William and Coleridge and in relation to Sarah.'

'I think you're probably right.'

There was a pause.

'OK, I think you are almost definitely right,' I said.

There was a further pause.

'Or even... just right.'

She laughed at my exaggerated respect for her point of view given our earlier conversation about Sarah on the walk. I knew there was more to come.

'You know, when I studied this, I was mainly researching the relationship between Coleridge and Sarah, but the fact is that Dorothy was not just as important in terms of the emotional and practical support she gave William, she was also an important literary influence - despite the fact that she was denied a formal education.'

'Which Sarah Coleridge was not.'

I got another 'hmm' as my reward.

'I don't think you should be too hard on Sarah,' she continued.

'I wasn't meaning to be. I was just trying to illustrate the difference between the undoubted physical and emotional support that Sarah Coleridge gave to Coleridge as opposed to the literary support that Dorothy undoubtedly gave to William.'

'Yes well, you do have a point, or at least it is a point that has often been expressed except...well it was quite heartless the way he abandoned her for the Hartz mountains.'

'Very good, Esther: heartless and Hartz mountains.'

Coleridge and the Wordsworths had taken a trip to Germany.

While Coleridge found the trip stimulating and immersed himself in German literature and philosophy, eventually enrolling as a student at the University of Gottingen, the Wordsworths became homesick and came home while Coleridge extended his stay. Sarah was originally due to go with them, but this proved impractical once their second son Berkeley was born. When Berkeley died in February 1799, rather than hurry home, Coleridge prolonged his stay and did not return until July.

'But it was heartless,' Esther continued. 'At the very moment she needed him he was not there for her. His problem was that he could not face up to the reality of the situation – that was no good for Sarah.'

'But he was remarkable in his own way.'

'Remarkable, yes, but distinctly flawed.'

'You see, I was trying to talk about Wordsworth and here we are talking about Coleridge and Sarah again. But I must admit, the more I discover about Coleridge the more I am fascinated by him. His life was a kind of Odyssey, full of periods of intense creativity and despair, full of personal and financial hardships, not to mention his struggle with addiction. '

'A kind of metaphorical Odyssey.'

'What about the person from Porlock'? Do you think that person ever existed?'

"Kubla Khan", vying with "The Rime of the Ancient Mariner" as Coleridge's best-known poem, reputedly would have been longer if the person from Porlock had not interrupted him while he was writing it. The story went that Coleridge had written the poem while under the influence of opium at a local farm, often thought to be Ash Farm, which I would be passing on the walk the following day. The whole of the poem, he claimed, was in his head and was ready to pour out on the page until that fateful interruption. When the visitor had gone, he could no longer remember the rest of the details of the poem.

'He or she may have existed,' said Esther, 'but I think it's fanciful to think the reason he could not finish the poem was because of that. I know that Coleridge had a reputation for dashing things off quickly, but I don't think it really works like that. Poetry, like prose, is something that you work at and refine. I don't think you can just pluck it out of the air.'

'Yes, the number of times I've had a dream and can't quite remember it except that it was really good. It's a great story though.'

'Talking of dreams, and much as I am enjoying our little discussion, we have an early start tomorrow if I'm to make that bus.'

Esther was to get an early bus to Minehead and then a bus to Washford where she would walk to The Valiant Soldier and be reunited with Aggie's Lambretta.

I told her that I would give her ten minutes to get herself sorted and then I would join her. When I finally did, slipping into the bedroom as quietly as I could, she was fast asleep. The journey, the long walk, the wine and fresh air had done its job. I tiptoed around before taking to my own bed in the corner hoping that I did not snore. My legs ached a little from the two days of walking, but it was a satisfying kind of tiredness, and I found myself looking forward to the walk the next day, despite the fact that Esther would not be with me.

14

I waited with Esther at the bus stop the next morning. We had eaten an early light breakfast and the pub had provided us with some cheese and pickle sandwiches to take on our respective journeys.

'I wish I could walk with you today,' she said. 'I did so enjoy it yesterday.'

'So did I.'

The bus pulled up, and she gave me a peck on the cheek.

'Let me know that you have arrived safely.'

'You too.'

After the bus had left, I continued my trek and retraced my steps back up the hill that we had descended the previous evening. Then I took a bridleway path. This was, according to the guide, going to be the steepest ascent of the entire route and it proved to be a real test of my stamina.

I stopped for a rest when I came to the first way marker. Afterwards, I turned left, still climbing but more gently now. Then the path changed direction once more and I found myself in a steep upward trajectory. I was breathing heavily, willing myself to carry on. Eventually I came to a T-junction where I was grateful for yet another rest. I turned right and embarked on a further climb. I dug in hard, looking at the ground rather than looking ahead, so as not to dispirit myself. After what seemed like an age, I reached Worthy Manor Toll Road. I took another left along the road, which was mercifully relatively flat, before going uphill along Pitt Lane. I felt a great sense of relief when I arrived at a junction and was instructed to turn sharp right where there were signs to Countisbury and Lynmouth and where the road began to take me downhill. However, my relief was short lived as the road once more took an upward curve. At Yarnor I continued straight past the farm drive and soon began descending towards Ash Farm.

Ash Farm has never been proven to be the place where Coleridge wrote "Kubla Khan" and was interrupted by the person from Porlock, but it has been considered to be the most likely candidate and is frequently mentioned as such (presuming the incident did in fact take place). I was surprised that, though there was a clear sign for Ash Farm, there was no plaque or sign recognising the Coleridge connection. The guide simply told me to carry on past the drive.

I ascended once more before dropping down to a stream at Culbone Combe. I passed Parsonage Farm beneath the plantation on top of Culbone Hill. I walked between high hedges as the path opened out again and wended its way around the hill to another stream at Withy Combe. At Silcombe Farm there was the option to take a detour to Culbone Church, reportedly the smallest church still in use in England. Despite the fact that I had a lot of miles to cover to finish my journey, it was, according to the guide, only a short detour, so I decided to take it.

The walk to the church was by means of a steep and winding downward path through a landscape dominated by straight growing sessile oaks and, when I arrived, I did not regret my decision. St Beuno's is a charming church with a small steeple on top of a pitched roof on about the same scale as a large chimney. In one corner there was a Jacobean boxed pew for the occupiers of Ashley Combe House where the English mathematician Ada Lovelace often stayed in the summer. I wondered if she used the pew when she stayed. I would shortly after be visiting Oare Church which was the setting of the infamous shooting of Lorna Doone during her marriage to John Ridd in the fictional romance, *Lorna Doone* by R. D. Blackmore (albeit based on real historical characters and incorporating some real events). However, it was Culbone Church that was used for a BBC series of the book. It was also significant because it was reportedly the place where Coleridge was visiting before he left for Ash Farm, or whichever farm it was, and wrote "Kubla Kahn".

In the corner as you enter the church was what I took to be an organ but on closer inspection discovered was a harmonium, operated through pumping foot pedals at the same time as you play and which crucially does not require electricity as the church is not connected to the grid and is lit by candles. I wished Esther was here as she played the piano. I had never seriously studied the piano but could rattle out a few tunes which I had learnt by heart. The only one I could call to mind at that moment was the James Bond theme. I was only able to produce a poor imitation of the tune and gave up after a few attempts, unhappy with how I was disrupting the calming atmosphere of the church.

I walked up towards the chancel, took some photos and examined the Bible. I thought of Esther. She was a Christian, I knew, but did not profess to be a member of any faith. Would she have prayed at this moment? I had no belief, but I liked the quietness and stillness and contented myself with thinking about Esther and secretly hoping that one day she might profess her love for me. I supposed it was praying of a kind.

I returned to the path and made my way to the next combe, Holmer's Combe, and then on to another combe at the delightfully named Twitchen. I crossed another stream and then descended to a road and another farm, Broomstreet Farm, another candidate, I had read, for the farm where "Kubla Khan" had been written. Another climb was followed by a steep and glorious descent among panoramic views to a road where I picked up a public footpath signposted to Oare. I felt duty bound to make the short detour to Oare Church as I had done to the church at Culbone. It is a larger church than Culbone but no less delightful with its unusual three bay nave. This is also the church where R. D. Blackmore's father was a rector.

This was the moment, I decided, as I sat on the church steps after my visit, to indulge in a cheese and pickle sandwich and coffee. Esther had thoughtfully loaned her flask to me for the rest of the journey and the landlord had topped it up with piping hot coffee that morning when he made us the sandwiches. I sent Esther some images of the two churches I had visited and wished her well on her journey.

After a few minutes, I again felt the pressure of time and soon returned to the Coleridge Way path and started making my way to Yenworthy. From here I passed Oaremead Farm and then followed a bridleway to the river and a riverside path through the valley to Glebe Farm before taking a footpath into Ashton Cleave. Once again I climbed steeply through trees before emerging onto open ground high above the valley. Following a sign for Brendon I crossed a stream at a footbridge. This was a rewarding part of the walk as I was still on high ground way above the valley and yet the route was relatively easy.

I finally made a descent towards a road. I crossed and passed behind gorse bushes and down a set of wooden steps before reaching a further road above Hall Farm. Following signs to Rockford and Watersmeet I eventually emerged at the Rockford Inn. There was no time to stop. I pushed on north towards Watersmeet. In several places there were spectacular examples of water cascading past and crashing onto rocks. The sound it made was at the same time curiously soothing and invigorating. At times the track veered away from the riverbank until the rushing water could no longer be heard, though always, at some point, it returned to the bank, as it did when I neared Watersmeet House.

I was tempted to stop at the well-stocked café and flirted with the idea of a cream tea but, in the end, compromised with a delicious ice cream which I ate as I continued my journey on the east bank of the river.

After I had finished my ice cream I sat on a rocky outcrop at the side of the river bank and took a few moments to read my guide. The name Watersmeet, I read, comes from the fact that the East Lyn River is joined by Hoar Oak Water and Farley Water and where the three rivers meet is a glorious site. In 1952, though, there was a year of unprecedented rain when nine inches of rain fell on the high ground in 24 hours. Catastrophic flooding followed. Large boulders and rocks were swept through Lynmouth and destroyed houses, roads and bridges with 34 people losing their lives. My guide also told me that this is the largest area of oak woodland in southwest England. There is a particular variety of Whitebeam that is only found on the Exmoor coast. This was also the home to the wonderfully named plant the Irish Splurge which is only found on one other site in mainland Britain.

I carried on through Horner's Neck Wood and then to Wester Wood continuing along a high path well above the water. There were more spectacular examples of water dashing along below me. It felt like a great adventure, and I wished Esther was still with me. Eventually, the north bank of the river brought me to the A39 main road. I crossed the road to the footbridge by a hotel before crossing the river and reaching the pier and the Exmoor National Park Visitor Centre in Lynmouth. This is the official end of the Coleridge Way, but my walk did not to end here as I wanted to walk the extra part to The Valley of the Rocks. However, in order to celebrate my achievement, I sat on the steps nearby and ate my remaining sandwich. I took a ten-minute rest and a few good swigs from my water bottle.

I texted Esther to say that I had finished the journey and that I was going to walk the extension. I felt as though I wanted to include her in the moment. I was rewarded with an instant reply. 'Well done. I hope you enjoy The Valley of the Rocks. Let's talk later.'

There was one other diversion I had decided on before I continued on my path and that was to travel on the Lynton and Lynmouth Cliff Railway. It is a funicular railway that runs between the two villages, Lynton at the top and Lynmouth at the bottom and is the steepest totally water powered railway in the world (5500 feet between the two stations) – and one of only three examples.

I had read up on its history the evening before. It had been entirely built by manual labour and was originally designed for transporting goods between the two settlements. However, it became a tourist attraction and was adapted for passenger use. No local power is required to operate the railway which means it has a low carbon footprint. Water is piped from the West Lyn River to a reservoir at the upper station. Once passengers are loaded, water is released from the bottom car until the top car is heavier than the bottom car and begins to descend, pulling the bottom car up as it does so. When the bottom car reaches the top, it is filled with water ready for the next descent. Halfway up is a passing bay where the tracks are separated allowing the two cars to pass each other. *Almost like a perpetual motion machine*, I thought. I made a mental note to tell Simon, though a funicular railway in his back garden, I thought, was beyond even him.

Taking the journey up to the top of the hill also saved me the steep walk upwards, which zig-zagged backwards and forwards over the route of the railway. There were seven other people in my railway car, including a dog and two excited children who kept swapping positions on the seats not knowing which way to look to get the best view. The views as we ascended were stunning as more of the bay and cliffs came into sight. When the cars passed each other at the passing point, children waved to children. There were smiles. A young man with dark Latin features looked straight at me and then away when he saw that I was also looking in his direction. When we exited the car, I found my way to the Southwest Coast Path which would take me to the Valley of the Rocks.

Eventually, I passed the front of Holiday Hill and then took a path to the left which took me to The Warren and to the shelter at Poets' Corner. It included examples of poetry by the illustrious visitors to the Valley of the Rocks, including Shelly and Southey, as well as Wordsworth and Coleridge.

I glanced at the time. I was due to meet Jonathan Sutcliffe of the Coleridge Society at 7.30 pm. He had suggested that we meet close to the benches by the second car park, a little further on from Poets Corner, and identified a spot where you could look at the landscape through a pay to view telescope not far from some benches. He gave me a phone number to use if, for any reason, he had not arrived by 7.30. It was now 7.10. Enough time for a bit of a wander, I thought, before our meeting.

The Valley of the Rocks was carved out during the ice age and runs parallel to the coast. As I came to the large rocky outcrop known as Castle Rock with its epic views of the sea, I began to appreciate that feeling that so many people had, including Coleridge and Wordsworth, of being in an otherworldly landscape. It was Robert Southey's description of the area that I had found the most evocative when he described the valley as 'the very bones and skeletons of the earth.'

I walked past the second car park and approached the benches close to Castle Rock and was met by a brown and white goat. I put my hand out to stroke its back. It resisted my gesture and moved away but not very far, wary but not entirely afraid of human contact.

To my left was another distinct rock outcrop where some brave souls had climbed to the top and were looking out to sea. I followed the path to the right and saw the telescope that Jonathan had mentioned. I strolled a little further along the well-made path. There were striking rock formations wherever I looked; rocks perched at impossible angles, caves and sink holes.

Coleridge, as I knew from my reading, was a frequent visitor and in 1797 Coleridge and Wordsworth had visited together. It inspired them to begin writing a story called "The Wanderings of Cain". Though it was never finished it marked an increasing collaboration between the two with Coleridge going on shortly after to write "The Rime of the Ancient Mariner". The following year marked the publication of *Lyrical Ballads*. Though they would both eventually move to the Lake District, this was the place where their ideas about being at one with nature began to develop and began to be expressed strongly through their poetry. For that moment, I was content to stand there on the edge of the world (as it seemed to me) taking it all in.

I am not great with heights, but I was drawn to the cliff edge not wanting to miss out on the magnificent views. I went as close to the edge as I dared as it seemed each step closer to the edge brought some new aspect of the scenery into view. I spent some time absorbing the beautiful craggy landscape and impossibly steep cliffs stretching out to a silver sea and experienced a sudden rush of positive energy and a feeling of well-being. I walked closer still to the edge. A gentle warm breeze enveloped me and my thoughts turned towards an evening of food and wine and (I hoped) of convivial friendship. Esther would not be with me but in a mysterious way I could still feel her presence.

At that moment I heard a noise and turned my head to see a man right behind me.

'Jonathan?' I said.

The man did not answer and without warning I felt him grab at my rucksack which I had draped over one shoulder. I instinctively resisted without being fully able to turn myself completely around and face him, precariously placed as I was near the edge of the cliff. The rucksack was yanked from me as he pushed me back with tremendous force. I was bundled into the air away from the cliff. I found myself in space between ragged rocks and a choppy sea and felt the expectation of my own body impaled upon the rocks below.

For a moment I was flying past the edge of the craggy cliff face. A gnarled root of a gorse bush appeared in view slightly proud of the cliff. I grabbed at it with my right hand and, finding a little purchase, then with my left. My body slammed against the side of the cliff. I felt my hands slipping away from the root and the root itself shuddered, loosening itself from the side of the cliff, but I hung on and, for that moment at least, the bush remained in its precarious position.

This felt like it was my only chance. I pressed myself against the cliff, taking a breath. The momentum of falling had stopped but I still felt the pull of gravity and an overwhelming inclination to fall. I glanced up at the rocky incline looking for a way out and saw the figure striding away with my bag. In my brief view of his face in the moment before he had pushed me, I realised that the person who had attacked me was the very man I had seen looking across to me on the cliff railway.

I needed to make forward and upward momentum somehow. A few feet above me, I could see a small ledge protruding from the cliff wall. I reached upwards with my right hand, but it was too much of a stretch and I momentarily fell back. It took all my strength to regain the crab-like position against the cliff and stop myself from falling backwards.

I tried once more and, with lots of determined scrambling, finally made it within reach of the small ledge. I just needed to negotiate a couple of hand holds and I would be back at the top. I forced myself upwards using all the strength I could muster in my aching arms. At last, I was able to drag myself over the top of the cliff edge. I sat down and began to tremble with emotion. I put my head in my hands.

Then there was a voice behind me.

'Elliot?'

I turned around.

'I couldn't find you by the benches, so I thought I had better stroll a bit further … are you all right?'

'I'm afraid something terrible has happened, Jonathan.'

15

I explained as best as I could, but my words came out all garbled. When at last I was able to relate my story, it took us both a while to take it all in.

'You poor chap. Here, take a breather for a moment. Perhaps away from the cliff edge?'

He led me over to a seat where we sat down together. I could not help putting my head in my hands again.

'I think you need to contact the police,' he said at last.

'I'm not sure if it was a deliberate effort to injure me. I think he was more interested in my rucksack.'

'Even so, he assaulted you – and he stole your rucksack.'

Jonathan had spotted the rucksack abandoned further along the cliff edge in the opposite direction to that he had come from, with some of its contents scattered along the path. He gathered them up and put them back in the rucksack and brought them over to me. I looked through them.

'I can't see that there is anything missing. My driving licence is still there but it looks like my credit card has gone. And my Richard Holmes book, that's gone too.'

'So, we're looking for a literary thief.'

'Yes.'

We both laughed. The humour was a relief for me at that moment.

I reached inside my pocket. My phone, miraculously, was still there. It had been in my pocket during the time I was bundled over the cliff. I rang the police.

'Did you see it? Did you see him push me?' I asked Jonathan as I held on to be put through.

'I'm sorry, I think I must have arrived just after it had happened. Did you get a good look at him yourself?'

'Just for the briefest moment from the back as he strode off with my rucksack. Tallish, dark hair. I think a grey jacket and jeans. The funny thing is, I think I saw him earlier when I took the Cliff Railway.'

Then there was a voice on the phone. 'Putting you through.'

I explained about the incident and gave the location of the car park. A car was in the area and would be with us shortly, I was told.

'It's good they are coming right away,' Jonathan said. 'Well, welcome anyway.' He shook my hand. 'Let's try and put all this behind us.'

'Yes, I don't want it to spoil my visit. I've had a great time so far on the walk and am really looking forward to learning more about Coleridge. It's so kind of you to put me up.'

'Not at all.'

'I'd better cancel my credit card, too.'

Once I had got through to the credit card company and a lengthy security check to establish who I was, the card was blocked and cancelled.

A nagging thought kept presenting itself in my head.

'You don't suppose the thief thought I had *Lyrical Ballads* with me?'

'But you sent it on ahead.'

'That's what I did but I think if you looked on my Facebook Page, the implication is that I was bringing it with me.'

'He took your Richard Holmes book. Perhaps he thought that was *Lyrical Ballads.*'

'*Lyrical Ballads* is in two volumes - but, then, there is no reason he would know that. Or he could just be a madman who took against me.'

At that moment a police car arrived. After I had explained the situation as best I could, the two police officers asked me to show them where the incident took place. Jonathan also accompanied us. It was starting to become dark now as we looked over the edge of the cliff at the place where I was attacked. All seemed tranquil apart from the sound of a goat bleating and the cry of a lone gull. It was difficult to believe that anything untoward had happened there at all.

They asked me if I knew my attacker. I related how I did not know him but that I thought it was the same man that I had seen in the Cliff Railway carriage. Then we talked about the contents of the rucksack and the fact that only the book had been stolen and one credit card but not my driving licence. They asked if I would mind coming to the station and making a statement.

Jonathan excused himself and phoned his wife.

'I'm sorry, I'm keeping you from your meal,' I said.

'It's fine,' he told me. 'It's the sort of meal that will keep. We can have supper instead of dinner.'

'You should go and join your wife,' I said.

But he said he felt honour-bound to accompany me to the station. In any case, at this stage, he was being treated as potentially being a witness to the incident given that he was on the spot shortly after it had happened.

When I made my statement at Lynton Police Station about 20 minutes later, motive of course came up.

Detective Constable Cliff Sanders interviewed me.

'Is there any reason why this gentleman might have attacked you?'

'The only reason I can think of,' I said, 'other than that he was looking for money or a phone or credit cards, is that he may have thought I was carrying a valuable book. My employee at my bookshop has been advertising the fact that I was taking a rare book to Somerset on Facebook. I realise now that this may not have been a sensible idea. In fact, I wasn't actually carrying that book but had sent it on ahead by courier. I did have a book in my rucksack, which he took, but it has no great value.'

'Yes, well, the card itself could be valuable for a few contactless transactions and, if you had a driving licence or passport, he may have been able to steal your identity. It is, sadly, becoming increasingly common and – I don't want to be indelicate sir – but if he did want you out of the way it would be convenient. You would not be cancelling your cards or reporting the loss of your ID.'

'When you put it like that, it has a really sinister logic to it.'

'I understand, though, that he took your card and not your driving licence.'

'Yes, and that book. I have blocked and cancelled my card.'

'This book then... *Lyrical Ballads*.'

'Yes, *Lyrical Ballads*.'

'How much did you say you thought it was worth?'

'Three to four thousand pounds.'

'A tidy sum for a book.'

It was indeed, but nothing like the value of the *First Folio* of Shakespeare which I had been involved in tracing the year before. I thought it best not to mention that – at least not at this stage.

'Were you bringing it down here to the Coleridge people to sell it?' he continued.

'No, I was bringing it down here as a gift. There was to be a presentation.'

There was a pause while he considered this.

'I hope you don't mind me asking, that's a lot of money to be giving away. Do you make a lot of money as a bookseller?'

I laughed involuntarily.

'You're right, I don't make a lot as a bookseller. It's often a struggle to make ends meet. A fellow bookseller once said to me: *How do you become a millionaire as a bookseller?*'

'And what was the answer?'

'*Start off as a billionaire.*'

It took him a moment, but he got there.

'That's very good, sir. I might use that myself.'

I had been avoiding mentioning the reason why I was giving the book away and how I came into possession of it in the first place. It was a complicated story, after all.

'The truth is I was given it by another bookseller, in Italy, but I was not comfortable with it as I suspected it may have been stolen.'

'Shouldn't you have reported it as such?'

'I did. In fact, I asked if I could send it back to whomever or wherever it came from. I have been in touch with the Italian police about this, but it seems that they can find no record of it being stolen.

'Ah, yes, I see.'

I could see that he was not absolutely convinced and was perhaps a little suspicious of my motives.

'I do have the details of the investigating officer in Italy,' I added.

'That could be useful.'

'In fact, I'm worried that this Italian bookseller may have been behind the attack on me.'

It was a recent thought but one that had become increasingly to the forefront of my mind.

'Even though he gave you the book in the first place?'

'I think he may have been trying to buy my silence about his relationship to someone whom I had seen him with, a Mr Abruzzio, who was later murdered. But I had already spoken to the police and mentioned the relationship.'

I explained about the theory that he was stealing books from the local library and passing them onto Cantalbrini for money for his daughter's cancer treatment in America.

'Can I take you back to the incident of when you were attacked, sir?'

'Yes.'

'You say you were just standing there, looking out to sea.'

'Yes, I had just finished the Coleridge Way and wanted to do this last bit – the extension to the Valley of The Rocks as I had heard it was very beautiful, and it was also a place I knew Coleridge and Wordsworth – the authors of the book - liked to visit.

'I agree sir, it is a very nice spot for us to have right on our doorstep. This man who attacked you. You said you got a look at him. He was not the bookseller you acquired the book from?'

'No, I'd never seen him before. I can't say I got a really good look at him. I thought I recognised him from when I took my trip on the cliff railway. He was thin and had the same hair, dark and short. It made me think he might be Italian.'

'It's strange isn't it. There you are just admiring the view, and someone comes and pushes you off the edge of the cliff, someone you have never seen before – at least, until that day.'

There was an element of scepticism in his voice that I was uncomfortable with.

'Yes, very. But I wonder if he was connected in some way to the bookseller.'

'You mean a kind of henchman or associate?'

'Yes, I suppose I do.'

'And you think he might have travelled all the way from Italy to try to get it back.'

'Either that or he may have been a contact who was already in the UK.'

'There wasn't a fight. You weren't in any kind of struggle – before you fell over the edge?'

'No, only in the sense that when I felt a tug at my rucksack I tried to keep hold of it. But then he pulled harder at the rucksack and pushed me. I'm not sure if he really meant to push me off the cliff. I think he was just intent on stealing my rucksack. It all happened so quickly.'

'And when you were pushed off the cliff – whether he meant it or not - you somehow managed to break your fall?'

'I managed to cling on to the root of a bush that was growing out of the cliff face. And then managed to scramble back up to the top. Shortly after that Jonathan came along.'

Following the interview, I made my written statement. I took some time going over it. I wanted to get it right. I signed it and was told I could leave with Jonathan.

'You are free to go, sir, but please be available in case of any new developments. You may also be asked to try and identify your attacker with some facial identification software that we have.'

'Does that mean I can attend the Coleridge event tomorrow?'

'I see no reason why not, unless as I say, there are any new developments. Make sure you are available to be contacted, though.'

16

Any lingering doubts about being welcome and the inconvenience I was causing were dispelled when Jonathan's wife Dora gave me a hug when Jonathan and I arrived at their house.

'How awful for you.'

My phone rang at that moment. Esther was trying to call me.

'So sorry I said,' and declined the call.

'Dinner has become supper,' she said. 'But I was preparing for a meal that could be a moveable feast, in any case, and I was not sure if you are vegetarian.'

She had prepared jacket potatoes, salad, ham, cheese, pork pie, beetroot and a variety of pickles.

'Perfect,' I said. 'Is it OK if I use the loo?'

'Of course, and Jonathan will show you the room. It has its own bathroom.'

I did not feel ready to talk to Esther about the incident so, once I was shown to my room, I sent her a quick message to say that I was fine (even if it was not strictly true) and that I would contact her in a little while.

I returned downstairs to Jonathan and Dora.

'I was wondering, Jonathan, if you still wanted to go ahead with the presentation,' I said as I tucked into a baked potato, suddenly appreciating how hungry I was. 'You may want to abandon the idea of being gifted the book after all.'

For Dora's benefit I explained about my meeting with Cantalbrini and the circumstances in which I had received it as a gift.

'I'll speak to the chairman and the secretary tomorrow,' said Jonathan, 'but my own feeling, for what it's worth, is that we need to be brave enough not to be put off by these awful circumstances. After all, you're the one who is on the right side of the law. It's not as though *you* have been going round attempting to push people off the top of a cliff. And I don't see that the society is in any danger.'

'I just don't want you to be put into a difficult position.'

'OK, let's see what my colleagues say in the morning.'

There was a moment of silence. I think all three of us were trying to take in the unusual situation.

'This is a lovely spread,' I said to Dora, not enjoying being left to my own thoughts.

'It's nothing really.'

'What's it like being part of the Coleridge Society? Must be interesting.'

Husband and wife smiled at each other.

'I guess you're both members, are you?'

'Yes, we are,' Dora said.

'We're smiling because sometimes our exchanges get quite heated,' said Jonathan. 'You wouldn't think so with something as sedate and worthy sounding as the Coleridge Society.'

I thought of an event in my bookshop the year before: a Shakespeare talk which had ended in a murder, and of the inflamed passions of the two academics involved, but thought it best not to mention it. Instead, I turned to my recent discussion on Coleridge with Esther.

'Yes, I do know. My colleague at the bookshop, Esther, had a heated discussion with me about Sarah Coleridge and Coleridge's treatment of her.'

There were more looks of recognition between the two.

'Yes, well,' said Dora, 'we have had that very discussion ourselves. I think Sarah was treated dreadfully while Jonathan is a bit more forgiving of STC.'

'I am not exonerating him completely,' said Jonathan. 'It's just, you can't deny his genius – and he did have mitigating circumstances.'

'It doesn't sound too dissimilar to our discussion.'

'Yes, STC seems to divide people like that... sorry, I always call him STC,' said Dora. 'He didn't like his own name, Samuel, and preferred to be called STC so we do the same. It's kind of a society thing.'

'Just like he didn't like Sarah with an "h",' I said.

I had learned this from my recent reading. Sarah Coleridge

dropped spelling her name with an 'h' because Coleridge preferred the name that way.

'Yes, some strange psychology operating there,' said Jonathan.

'And, of course, there was the other Sara,' said Dora.

This was Sara Hutchinson, the younger sister of Mary Hutchinson (who came to stay with the Wordsworths when they were at Racedown and, eventually, became Wordsworth's wife). Coleridge fell in love with Sara in 1799 when he met her while staying with the Wordsworths at Thomas Hutchinson's farm near Darlington. But then, Coleridge always seemed to be falling in love. Before he married Sarah Fricker, he was in love with Mary Evans from a family he knew from Christ's Hospital, the boarding school he attended in London after his father died.

'Yes, I'm sure you're aware, the other Sara was otherwise known as Asra,' said Jonathan.

'That was his secret name for her,' said Dora. 'And he refers to her often in his poetry and notebooks. In many ways she was a good friend to him though his affection was not fully returned.'

'There was no evidence that their love was consummated, and she remained unmarried,' continued Jonathan.

'Ah, I had heard something about that but have not got that far in my Richard Holmes book – and I guess I won't for a while now that my copy has been stolen.'

'Now I can help you there. Join me in my Coleridge Library.' I followed him over to a bookcase in the corner about four shelves high. It contained nothing but books about Coleridge.

'Ah, yes, here we are.'

He plucked out a copy of *Early Visions* which was next to the second volume entitled *Darker Reflections* concerning Coleridge's later life, which was also on my reading list. And there was so much more: biographies of Coleridge by Rosemary Ashton, Molly Lefebure, Oswald Doughty and Adam Nicolson; of Coleridge and Wordsworth specifically in the West Country by Berta Lawrence and Tom Mayberry, and also of Sarah Coleridge – and a whole load of Coleridge Digests produced by The Coleridge Society.

'What an amazing collection!'

'I think only the library in Nether Stowey has more,' said Dora with a hint of pride.

'What I find fascinating is the amount of other interesting events and people that come out of this part of Somerset,' I said.

'Well, yes, you could write a whole other book about that and, quite a few of them with links to Coleridge and the Nether Stowey area. What had you in mind?'

'Well, earlier, we were having a discussion about the Walford murder,' I said.

'Yes, well I think we can all agree,' said Dora, 'that Jane Shorney has often been represented shamefully. I think recent thinking on that has changed considerably. There has been so much sympathy for John Walford as though he was the victim – forgetting the fact of how brutal a murder it was.'

'Yes, I think I can agree with that,' said Jonathan. 'I guess you know the story.'

'Horrific,' I agreed.

'Yes, it was and yet over the years he has elicited much sympathy for being caught by this "conniving" woman,' said Dora.

'I wonder if now she would have been considered to have learning difficulties,' said Jonathan.

'Which makes it even more shameful,' said Dora.

'I walked past the spot where I believe he was hanged. I suppose the sympathy part comes from the fact that he almost married Ann Rice?'

'Yes,' continued Dora. 'Ann Rice, who was from a good local family. The story goes that they were very much in love but were prevented from marrying because of his mother's resistance to the marriage. They got as far as reading the bans before the marriage was abandoned. Walford then took up with Jane Shorney and married her when she became pregnant by him. However, Ann had also become pregnant by Walford and gave birth to a daughter in November 1789, only three months after the hanging. She died in February 1790 leaving the daughter orphaned. This is where a lot of the sympathy for him comes from, I think. There was undoubtedly an element of tragedy there.

'But, even so,' said Jonathan. 'That murder was very brutal.'

'Did he admit to the murder?' I asked.

'He tried to deny it at the beginning,' said Jonathan. 'And here's an interesting thing, Thomas Poole senior, the father of Thomas Poole who was such good friends with Coleridge – he was the one that investigated John Walford. He had known him most of his life. And he prosecuted him for murder.'

'And did Coleridge know him?'

'Poole told him about the murder, but he didn't know Walford as far as we are aware,' said Dora.

'If we want to continue down this gruesome track,' said Jonathan, 'there was also the murder of Charles Lamb's mother by his sister.'

'Yes. I read about that in Holmes.'

'As you no doubt remember, Mary had a debilitating mental condition and stabbed her mother to death after she admonished her for being rude to a servant.'

'Yes, the remarkable thing about that,' continued Dora, 'is that because of Charles Lamb's efforts she avoided being convicted and hung. She was put into an asylum but eventually gained her freedom on the condition that Charles was always there to look after her. Quite enlightened by the standards of the time.'

'And they went on to write the wonderful *Tales from Shakespeare* together,' Added Jonathan.

'Anything I should know about that is not murder-related?' I asked.

'There's Andrew Crosse of Fyne Court. We might have time to go and visit there. And there are some amazing walks in the grounds. He was a scientist, who, incidentally, wrote poetry.'

'They often seemed to do both things then,' I said.

'Coleridge, of course, is a good case in point. He had an interest in the sciences and philosophy and metaphysics, as well as poetry,' said Dora.

'Crosse never met Coleridge though, did he?' threw in Jonathan.

'No, I don't think there is any evidence for that - but Crosse did know Robert Southey,' said Dora 'and took him for walks in the Quantocks.'

Jonathan took up the story of Andrew Crosse again.

'Crosse was an early pioneer of electricity but also there was one scandalous moment when he was vilified for playing God. He conducted an experiment that appeared to spontaneously create life.'

'That's some claim,' I said.

'It was an electrolysis experiment, and I'm not sure he ever believed it himself. I think he thought that there were eggs buried among the samples – but that did not stop the newspaper coverage,' said Jonathan.

'The other intriguing connection is Ada Lovelace,' said Dora.

'Ah, yes, wasn't she the first computer programmer?'

'It's contested by some but yes, working with Charles Babbage, there is evidence that she was certainly very influential in developing the early ideas around the programming of computers. She also knew Jonathan Faraday,' continued Dora. 'She was the daughter of Lord Byron though she never knew him. Byron and her mother Annabella separated two months after her birth. Then she married William who was a Baron and she became Lady King. They had their honeymoon at a house at Ashley Combe, not that far from Culbone Church. It had been built as a hunting lodge, and it became their summer retreat. Sadly, it went to ruin and was pulled down in the 70s.'

'Ah, yes,' I said. 'I remember seeing the private pews in the church where she was believed to have sat during the service.'

'And the significance of that vis-à-vis Coleridge is that it was Byron who persuaded Coleridge to publish "Kubla Khan" many years after he had written it,' said Jonathan. 'Sorry to take your punchline away from you, dear.'

She looked across at him. I was not sure if it was in a forgiving way or whether there was a flash of anger or irritation.

'This is all fascinating,' I said.

'And you heard about Joshua Toulmin that Coleridge preached for in Taunton?' said Jonathan.

'Yes, the lady at the Unitarian Church told me. He seems to have been a remarkable man in his own right.'

At that moment another thought occurred to me.

'I was forgetting. You said the *Lyrical Ballads* arrived safely.'

'Oh, yes, I'll fetch the package. I didn't open it,' said Jonathan. 'We thought we would wait for you.'

Jonathan was back in a moment.

'Shall I open it?' he asked me.

'Yes, why not? With everything going on it will be reassuring to know that it has arrived in good order.'

'I see you have packed it very well.'

'That was Esther.'

When the parcel containing *Lyrical Ballads* was at last opened, we showed extreme reverence for two little books, as they took pride of place at the centre of a small side table adjacent to the shelves of Coleridge books.

Dora hovered excitedly.

'Do you think we can have a peek inside?' she asked.

'Yes, why not.'

'Should we wear gloves?'

'No, the current thinking,' I said, 'is that gloves can do more harm than good. You can snag and tear the paper. The approach now is to use your hands but make sure they are clean and dry and have no moisturiser or cream on them.'

We all proceeded to the kitchen to wash our hands and dry them before we returned to the books.

'Perhaps if just one of us is responsible for the turning to the pages,' I said.

'Why don't you do it Dora?'

She turned the first pages.

'There are quite a few changes from the first edition. "The Rime of the Ancient Mariner" has now been moved to the back, last but one except for "Lines Written a few Miles Above Tintern Abbey", whereas it was at the front in the previous edition.' I had learned as much from Cantalbrini.

'I think Wordsworth thought it was affecting sales,' said Jonathan. 'I think the archaic words he used were considered a distraction from the new poetry they were trying to write. In later versions he removed a lot of the archaic words.'

'And Coleridge didn't object,' said Dora. 'I think he even agreed with Wordsworth. You have to remember that Coleridge was totally in awe of Wordsworth. He thought he was a greater poet and always felt inferior to him.'

'That's another bone of contention, I'm afraid,' said Jonathan. 'Coleridge was always in his shadow but Coleridge's encouragement and influence was critical in the development of Wordsworth's poetic style. You could claim that Wordsworth perhaps owed more to Coleridge than Coleridge ever did to Wordsworth.'

'And yet, it was Wordsworth's influence that helped Coleridge in the development of his poems as well,' said Dora. 'You only have to look at "Frost at Midnight" to look at the similarities of structure with "Tintern Abbey".'

'I just love listening to you two talking,' I said.

'Well, the Coleridge-Wordsworth thing is a subject that may well arise tomorrow in the talk. For now, I guess the most important thing for you is to get some well-earned rest,' said Jonathan.

'Yes, thank you, I will. Apart from the incident this evening my bones are a little weary from three days of walking.'

I went to bed feeling reassured by Jonathan and Dora's company and kind words and not a little stimulated by our discussions about Wordsworth and Coleridge.

It was nearly midnight following our late supper and discussion and, despite the fact that I was feeling tired, my brain would not switch off. I decided to distract myself by looking up Halsway Manor, the place where the annual conference about Coleridge was to be held, on my phone. It looked like an amazing location, best known for holding residential weekends and gigs on folk music - and set in beautiful countryside. I flicked through the website and caught glimpses of events in a room with high arched windows and chandeliers running down the middle.

I slept fitfully after that and could not help running the events of earlier in the day over-and-over in my head. I could not get the Walford murder and the violent attack on Jane Shorney out of my head.

Sometime later, the events at the cliff face came back to me during my sleep. This time, in my dream, I missed the gorse bush that I had grabbed when I was pushed over the cliff edge. I dropped through the air and hit the pebbles at the bottom of the cliff with a thump. I found myself looking up at the man who had pushed me, peering over the edge of the cliff and sneering at me. I woke up with a start, screaming and sweating. I took a drink of water and went to the bathroom. Then I heard a knock on my door. It was Jonathan.

'Elliot are you all right? I heard you shouting.'

'Yes, thank you.' I got out of bed and walked up to the door but did not open it. 'Just a bad dream that's all.'

I could see no sense in denying it.

'Thank you,' I said. 'I'll be all right now.'

However, I had trouble getting to sleep after that; afraid to sleep in case those disturbing visions returned. I listened on my phone to some classical music on radio 3. Mendelssohn's *Hebrides Overture* was playing, popularly known as "Fingal's Cave". Perhaps it was not the most appropriate music considering its coastal setting, but the beauty of the music helped calm me.

Later, when I did find sleep again, I found myself inside Halsway Manor. There were three magnificent chandeliers, beautifully arched windows and I was sitting on a platform with several other guests. Jonathan was reading "The Rime of the Ancient Mariner" with some type of classical music that perfectly accompanied it, though I could not say what that music was. He was reading from the copy of *Lyrical Ballads* I had donated, on a lectern with gloves on. I felt anxious. I was trying to say, 'We should not read from this original, we should be reading from a copy – and you should not be wearing gloves, you might tear the pages.' But it was as though my words were stuck inside my head, and I was unable to voice them. His hands kept turning the pages with what seemed to me was reckless abandon. His voice was otherworldly and sonorous, quite unlike his normal speaking voice. Then all at once he had finished. I felt relieved that he had stopped turning the pages and that they were no longer in danger of being torn.

Jonathan leaned across to me and said, 'Now you have to make your speech.'

All at once I was on my feet. 'It was an honour,' I said, 'and a great privilege.' Words flowed from me without effort, and I remembered enjoying the experience. Then a man stood up in the audience and shouted across at me.

'Is it right,' he said, 'that you should have taken the gift of my book and betrayed me? I have come here to take back the book that I now consider stolen. Omerta,' he shouted. 'You broke the silence.'

It was none other than Antonio Cantalbrini. He wore a Victorian cape and was supporting himself with an elegant silver embossed cane which he waved in my direction as he spoke.

'Now, Mr Todd,' he continued, 'I will take my revenge and may you rot in hell.'

He put his stick to one side, raised his arm at full length and fired from a pistol that he took from his pocket. The shot hit me full on the chest and a red patch immediately began expanding across my front. Once again, I was experiencing the feeling that I was about to die.

When I woke abruptly for the second time that night, I was shaking and dared not go back to sleep. I thought of phoning Esther but decided that it was wrong to trouble her at two in the morning. I remembered that I had not phoned her as I said I would. Perhaps I would ring her in the morning?

I switched on the light and returned to the radio and a programme about the evolution of copyright. It had the desired effect and led me to sleep, though rather fitfully, through the rest of the night. I could not help thinking that there might, in reality, be a connection between the incident on the cliff and Cantalbrini. Was it too far-fetched to think that he would attempt to retrieve the book that he had gifted me because I had betrayed him, if not in person, through one of his associates? I considered contacting Laura again.

Jonathan knocked on my door at eight and asked if I would join him for breakfast at nine. I was feeling tired following my disturbed night but had no wish to lay in bed any longer. There was a bath as well as a shower in my en-suite room. I took the opportunity of a long languorous bath, an attempt to soothe away the aches and pains of my walk. It also gave me time to think and consider the events of yesterday in the light of a new day. I tried to appreciate how lucky I was to escape harm rather than to dwell on it in a negative light.

Dora had to be somewhere early – a friend was in crisis and needed some reassuring words - so Jonathan and I breakfasted alone.

'Good news,' he said. 'I've contacted the other committee members, and they are unanimous in wanting the presentation to go ahead.'

'Oh, I'm pleased. I just didn't want to put you in a difficult position.'

'The only thing is… we don't want you to go ahead if you think it will be too much for you. Everyone is sympathetic with your plight and, I hope you don't mind, but I explained that it had rather shaken you and that you did not have a very good night.'

'No, that's OK. I don't mind.'

'One suggestion was that your gift could be acknowledged but you would not have to stand up on stage.'

'What do you think?'

'I think, if you're prepared to do it, as you have come all this way, it may make you feel better.'

'A way of exorcising my demons. My biggest fear now is that someone will try and steal *Lyrical Ballads*, if that was the original intention.'

'Well, we were thinking that we would put them on display in a small glass cabinet that we have, so that people could

come and look close up without damaging them in any way. I'm wondering if it would be good if we had a couple of guards either side.'

'A couple of bouncers from the Coleridge Society! Sorry,' I said immediately afterwards, 'I didn't mean to mock.'

'No offence taken. I know, it does sound a bit odd. I don't think we're known for our strong-arm tactics.'

'But it's a thought. The deterrent effect. Had you any particular people in mind?'

'I thought one of them could be my wife. I find her formidable so I can't see any reason why the potential assailant wouldn't.'

'Good choice, I think. I have decided I will be there on stage when the presentation occurs. Can't run away from these things.'

'That's settled then... we will, in fact, have quite a bit of time before things kick off later this afternoon.' He crunched on some toast. ' I was wondering whether you wanted to pop down to Ottery St Mary?'

'Where STC was born?'

'Yes, as we have recently had his 250th anniversary they have put up a statue to him.'

'I would like that.'

'We could do the walk from the church to Cadhay Bridge where he went missing overnight. It's only about a mile, I think. Do you know the story?'

'Yes, I remember reading about it in *Early Visions*. He was very young, wasn't he, to be spending a whole night on his own?'

'Only seven, I believe. You know he was the youngest of ten. He'd had an argument with one of his older brothers, Frank, who'd been bullying him. He pulled a knife on him. His mother scolded him. He was so upset that he ran away and stayed out all night.'

'That's quite a thing at that age.'

'Yes, emotionally, physically. There's evidence to support that it affected his health in later life. He suffered badly from rheumatic fever. It may be the reason he first started taking opium.'

'It was regularly taken for all sorts of ailments in those days, though, wasn't it?'

'Yes, by women, men, children. What may be have been even more traumatic for him was the death of his father a year later.'

'He certainly seems to have had a difficult early life.'

'I'm sorry you had such a bad night,' Jonathan said as we began our car journey.

'I'm sorry I disturbed you.'

'Not at all.'

'It all seems a bit unreal, I must admit. Anyway, I'm going to try and put it behind me and enjoy the day.'

Jonathan went on to describe some of his fellow members of the Coleridge Society. There was the 'Prof' *who knows more than anybody* (though I found it difficult to imagine that anybody knew more about Coleridge than Jonathan and his wife), and Alice, *the doyen of organisers* who knew when everything was happening and who should be doing what.

'Every organisation needs one of those,' I said.

There's also Desdemona,' said Jonathan. 'She's the one who keeps trying to tap into Coleridge's spiritual side. Most of us admire Coleridge from a distance but she is into experiencing things as though she was there.'

'Sounds like you have a very diverse range of people.'

'Well, you'll meet Desdemona and hear her read. She reads very intense versions of Coleridge's poems. Keep this to yourself but there have also been suggestions that she and a partner indulged in certain substances to mimic the Coleridge experience and that she even indulged before the performance of some of her poems. There was an unkind story going around that she had taken a drug dose to mimic the writing of "Kubla Khan" but had woken up and written nonsense. She was supposed to have said: *No bloody Xanadu for me and I wasn't even interrupted by the person from Porlock unless, you count the sound of my partner snoring.* But whether this was apocryphal or not, I'm not sure.'

'That's true dedication to your work.'

'Most of us, though, are a pretty ordinary bunch. All that we have is our love and admiration for an extraordinary man - for all his faults.'

'This is more like a cathedral than a church,' I said once we had parked and approached Saint Mary's church in Ottery.

'Yes, it's often described as a miniature cathedral. It's got two towers as well, which, apparently, is also unusual.'

The statue of Coleridge near the church entrance showed him in the prime of his life, in motion with open book in hand, walking on a rocky outcrop.

'I love the sense of movement,' I said.

'Yes, I think it's rather fine.'

I took the opportunity of having a photo taken with the great man and sent it on to Esther, apologising that I had not been in touch and saying all was fine. I could not bring myself to tell her about the attack on the edge of the cliff.

We went inside the church, as impressive on the inside as on the outside. It was fan-vaulted and had distinctive painted roof bosses.'

'Ha, I love those.'

I was looking at gaping men's mouths set in the ceiling.

'Do you know what they were for?' said Jonathan.

'To ward off evil spirits?'

'Well, that may well be right, but their immediate practical use was that they were the place where the bell-ringing ropes came through.'

We walked a little further.

I looked up at a large square blue clock.

'It's an astronomical clock based on Ptolemaic cosmology,' said Jonathan.

'The sun revolving around the earth.'

'Precisely.'

'It's one of the oldest surviving mechanical clocks in the country.'

'I bet Coleridge's dad must have loved being in charge of this church.'

'Yes. I believe he did. But it was also a magical playground for the young Samuel. And, of course, he had all the surrounding countryside as well.'

'I suspect it helped to foster his interest in nature.'

'He wrote about it in his poem "Frost at Midnight", one of the poems written at Nether Stowey.'

He began to recite:

oft
With unclosed lids, already I had dreamt
Of my sweet birthplace, and the old church tower,
Whose bells, the poor man's only music, rang,
From morn to evening, all the hot Fair-Day,
So sweetly, that they stirred and haunted me
With a wild pleasure, falling on my ear
Most like articulate sounds of things to come

'Bravo!' I exclaimed. 'I'm impressed that you remember it.'
'Thank you, but I wrote a paper on it for our *Coleridge Journal*. I became so familiar with it that it seems natural.'
'Even so, I'm still very impressed.'
'Shall we try that walk? We can go via the poetry stones.'
'Poetry stones?'
'I'll show you what I mean.'
We left the church and walked for a few minutes until we entered a park. The stones were to one side of the park and began spelling out the beginning of *Kubla Khan*. The words were spread over a number of stones. We began to read:

In Xanadu did Kubla Khan A stately pleasure-dome decree: Where Alph, the sacred river, ran Through caverns measureless to man Down to a sunless sea.

'There are 68 stones in all,' said Jonathan.
We walked the stones until we came to a very charming brick-built bridge.
'Would it have been like this when Coleridge was here?"
'There's been a bridge here since the 1500s but it was rebuilt after Coleridge's time.'
'It's a nice spot. I can see why he chose it. And he would have had some shelter under the arches if he wanted.'
'He retained a great fondness for it. He later wrote a sonnet called *To the River Otter*.'
'Oh, really.'
'Yes, he talks about skimming stones and the happy hours he spent here, but it is also mournful and regretful that he cannot experience those feelings anymore as he has all the

responsibilities of being an adult.'

'It's a lovely river. I can see why he liked it.'

After the walk we sat in the Silver Otter Café and had toasted teacakes and a pot of tea.

'You know there is another thing about Ottery Saint Mary that is notable,' said Jonathan.

'Oh, yes, what's that?'

'On Guy Fawkes Night they race down the streets with flaming tar barrels on their shoulders.'

'That sounds crazy.'

'It is!'

'It dates from the 17th century. They think it may have started as a means of warding off evil spirits.'

'So, what exactly happens?'

Though he was telling me, I found it hard to believe that it was allowed.

'They light these tar barrels outside the four pubs in town – though apparently there used to be 12 pubs. I think there are 17 barrels. Don't ask me why. They're really heavy, 30-kilogram barrels. Then they just race each other down the middle of the street like lunatics. You need to have been born in Ottery or lived here most of your life to compete and apparently there is a lot of competition between old established families.'

'Sounds even more crazy now that you've explained it to me.'

'It is! I have been a couple of times, and I have to say that you don't feel that safe as a spectator, never mind as a tar barrel runner – or whatever the correct term is.'

'Is it legal?'

'Well, I know the insurance keeps increasing each year. I think it's just such a unique and established tradition that no one wants it to end.'

'Reminds me of that thing in Gloucestershire where they fling themselves down a hill with a piece of cheese.'

'Well, that's probably just as crazy but at least there is no fire involved.'

I was quite sure in my own mind that I would not attempt to take place in either of these events if I was ever given the opportunity.

18

As we drove back from Ottery St Mary, Jonathan explained about the forthcoming events.

'There are two events this afternoon on Thomas Poole and Coleridge's opium use. They call them seminars but really, it's someone giving a short lecture and then taking questions from the audience. I am giving the first one. In the evening there are some poetry readings, music and the presentation and then, tomorrow, a lunch to close the event.'

'Sounds great!'

'I think the talk about Coleridge's addiction, or otherwise, might be quite lively. People tend to take sides on that one like they do with the Sarah debate. Thankfully, the Prof is doing that one and not me.'

When we returned to the house, we found Dora a little agitated.

'It's Desdemona's son. I mean, we have to be a bit careful about what we say. It's all in confidence...'

'What's happened?' asked Jonathan.

'The gist of it is that they had an argument and now he seems to have gone missing. It's quite a regular occurrence, but he usually sends her a text or some sort of message just to let her know he is OK.'

'Perhaps his phone's not charged,' said Jonathan.

'Yes, I suppose that's a good point.'

'It's always happening to me,' I said. 'I'm always losing my charger apart from anything else.'

'Just like Jonathan,' said Dora.

'Do you know what the argument was about?' asked Jonathan.

'She didn't say in detail but, you know, poor Cassio has not had the easiest time with his father leaving when he was so young. You wouldn't know he was from the same family. And this is where it's unusual perhaps to modern ears, it's the son accusing the mother of being too bohemian. Handsome as he is, Cassio is quite strait-laced. You wouldn't know that they were related.'

'Did you say he's called Cassio?' I could not help saying. 'Is that after Michael Cassio?'

'Yes.'

'Of course, he was Desdemona's admirer in Othello.'

'I'm afraid I would have to say, not always in this case,' said Dora.

'I think he prefers to be called Michael or Mike because it's more ordinary,' said Jonathan. 'I think he sees it as another one of his mother's foibles. But she always refers to him as Cassio.'

'I think I need a cup of tea before we go to the event,' said Dora. I could do with something stronger really.'

'That's OK, we've got time,' said Jonathan.

Jonathan and Dora both seemed a little distracted as we drank from a hastily prepared pot of tea. I tried to fill in the silence.

'You know my mother is taking a course on cults – she's studying them for her Open University project, especially the ones that involve community living. Apparently, while the parents are into free love and communal living, it's often the children who find it difficult and criticise the parents.'

'That's interesting. I'm not sure if Desdemona didn't experience some of this communal living in her youth,' said Dora.

'How long has he been out of contact?' asked Jonathan.

'About three or four days now.' She turned to me. 'He has this static caravan not far from here. It's a kind of compromise so that he can escape when he needs to and still has somewhere warm and dry. *Or shack with whoever he wants out of reach of his mother prying eyes.* That's what I've heard her say to him, but I know it makes him cringe and I don't think he sees it like that. They are so different,' she sighed. 'On top of it all, he has this terrible stutter when he is in a stressful situation.'

'Do you know if Des is still happy to do the readings?' asked Jonathan.

'She didn't say otherwise.'

'I guess she thinks that it may take her mind off it.'

'I'll be ready to step in if by any chance she doesn't show.'

'I suppose we'd better think about going shortly.'

'I'll sit in the back,' said Dora, 'and have a read through on the way – just in case.'

The first event of the afternoon was the one to be given by Jonathan on Thomas Poole and his role in supporting Coleridge and the village of Nether Stowey. We had the great privilege of having access to the house owned by Thomas Poole, now in private hands. Luckily, its owner was a member of the Coleridge Society. We walked from the Thomas Poole Library, where we were parked, and given a brief tour, including of the library with its barrel-vaulted roof.

After our tour of the house, we returned to our cars and drove the short distance to Halsway Manor where the talks were to take place. We had stayed a little longer than intended at Thomas Poole's house, so on arrival at Halsway we were directed immediately into the conference room ready for Jonathan's talk.

'The purpose of this talk,' began Jonathan, 'is not just to explain the importance of Thomas Poole in his relationship with Samuel Taylor Coleridge, but his importance in the life of the people of Nether Stowey generally, and farther afield, his relationships with and influence on other great men of the period.

'Most of us know that Thomas Poole was a great friend to the Coleridges and found them the cottage in Lime Street. However, what you may not know is the great extent of his philanthropy to other people in Nether Stowey and the community in general.

'It was made possible by the wealth he accumulated when he took over his father's tanning and farming businesses, which he improved and developed. He also developed other businesses, as a maltster buying from local growers and with a quarry on Castle Hill to provide stone for local buildings. The Doddington Copper mine which he also established was the one business that was never profitable, but overall, he accumulated considerable wealth.'

This answered a question I had when I had walked the

Coleridge Way and had wondered about the ownership of the Doddington Copper Mine.

'One of his greatest achievements was the building of the village school (now part of the library) built between 1812-13. It was one of the first free schools in the country offering education for up to 200 children.'

Jonathan continued to list Thomas Poole's achievements, often with accompanying slides. He had opened The Quantock Savings Bank to encourage the local population to save money and to give them access to banking, he provided bread for the starving and founded a female friendly society to offer financial aid to working women in times of sickness, hardship or old age. He was also a friend to Humphry Davy, The Wedgwoods, Charles Lamb, William Hazlitt, Robert Southey and Andrew Crosse. The fact that he was self-taught (his father refused to allow him to go to university) made his achievements even more remarkable.

Jonathan then went on to explain Poole's relationship with Coleridge, how he had been immediately impressed by him (like so many), found the cottage for the Coleridges (though to begin with it was a much grander property that failed to become available in the end) and remained a friend to both Samuel and Sarah, even after they had become estranged. He gave financial support for Coleridge's periodical *The Friend* and supported their son Hartley through Oxford.

When we went to questions, the discussion became the most animated when the subject of Coleridge and Sarah's relationship came up.

A Coleridge Society member called Dennis Chabon defended Coleridge, citing his belief that they were not a well-matched couple.

Desdemona stood up. She was incensed.

'Sarah was a remarkably well-educated woman, especially given the harsh circumstances she found herself in after her father's business fell into decline. The truth of the matter was that he married her in the first place to be a skivvy on the Susquehanna River, not as an equal partner and when that did not work out, she became a skivvy at their cottage, and he was completely heartless when he failed to return on the death of their son.' There was a noise from Desdemona's phone. 'I'm sorry, I have to go,' she said and disappeared through the back door near to where she was sitting.

It was not clear whether Desdemona had left through disgust at Dennis Chabon and his opinions or whether she had another reason for leaving. There was a tense moment before Jonathan broke the silence and attempted to smooth things over.

'I agree with much of what Desdemona said. I'm sorry that she's not able to stay as I do think it's important that we have these debates, however strong our feelings are in one direction or the other. My view, for what it is worth, is that I think we must judge him by the standards of the time. Even so, I think there is no doubt that he was lacking in empathy. There may be particular reasons why this was the case. It is suggested by some commentators that he had bi-polar disorder or ADHD and that this may have influenced his judgement and, of course there is the question of his addiction to opium. This is the subject of the next talk, so maybe we can leave it there and revisit it. Perhaps this will give us further insight into their relationship, among other things.

The meeting finished with applause for Jonathan who also praised the audience for their good questions There was also a lot of excited chatter afterwards, no doubt most of it regarding Desdemona's spirited performance and her dramatic exit.

A thirty-minute break for refreshments was announced with the details of the programme to follow: What was described as an exciting new acquisition (the *Lyrical Ballads* donation), a medley of music from C.H.H. Parry, Henry Smart, and Samuel Coleridge-Taylor through to modern day composers Richard Lloyd and Brian Daubney (to be played during the break). During the finale there would be the playing of Howard Skemton's musical version of "The Rime of the Ancient Mariner" with the poem sung by a baritone singer (Roderick Williams).

I stayed behind while preparations were made for the presentation which was to be held after the next talk. *Lyrical Ballads* was placed within the cabinet next to the front of the stage with pages open at the beginning of "The Rime of the Ancient Mariner". Dora was in attendance as was a burly young man whom I recognised from the audience. They were both wearing Hi-Vis jackets.

Following the break the Prof stood, unlike Jonathan, with his feet apart and no sign of any notes in front of the lectern. It was clear that he was going to take a different approach to delivering his talk.

'Before I start, because this is rather a long and involved subject, rather than have a lecture followed by a question-and-answer session in the usual way, please can I ask that you interrupt and make your points as they occur to you. We are rather limited for time given the vast amount of material on the subject and this will speed things along. We may have one or two questions at the end, but I would rather that we deal with most questions and opinions along the way. If we do not have time for your question, I am also happy for you to email me after the talk and I will get back to you. Just shout things out or put your hands up and I will moderate things if I need to. It may be a little chaotic, but I hope will make for a lively debate. So, here we go.'

He took a swig from a glass of water and cleared his throat.

'Any talk of the extent of Coleridge's addiction must be put into the context of the times. As I am sure you are aware, opium in the form of Laudanum, a solution of opium powder in alcohol, was widely used in eighteenth century Britain. It was used to treat everything from pain and insomnia to what were termed female disorders, or even to treat crying babies. When Coleridge started using opium is open to some dispute, but it is likely that he was given it from a young age, perhaps even as young as seven when he spent a night out in the open following an argument with one of his brothers and when he developed rheumatic fever. It's also clear that he was indulging in opium when he was at Cambridge as a student, following his time at Christ's Hospital, the boarding school he was sent to after his father had died. And, of course, once Thomas de Quincey published *Confessions of an English Opium Eater* in 1822, Coleridge's use of opium became public knowledge, whereas previously he had kept his drug taking as hidden as possible.

'Some biographers have played it down but there is one

thing we must be absolutely clear about, and that is that Coleridge had an addiction to opium, and he was as much a victim of this as any modern drug user. Many people, such as Southey, said that it was self-inflicted and tied it in with what they determined his laziness...'

'He still wrote better poetry than anything Southey did,' shouted someone from the audience, taking advantage of the invitation to interrupt. I thought of the flowery "Porlock"poem of Southey's I had read.

'And, one could argue,' continued the Prof, taking the interruption in his stride, 'achieved far more than Southey through his philosophical writings, his *Biographia Literaria* and through his analysis of the works of Shakespeare. It is also true that Coleridge received approbation for his addiction unlike, for example, William Wilberforce, the anti-slavery campaigner who was also addicted to opium.

'He also had intense moments of self-awareness. The letter that he wrote to Joseph Cottle suggested that he had been *seduced into the accursed habit ignorantly.* There is definitely an attempt at self-justification here, an attempt to exonerate himself from guilt but it is also true that he was not given the support he craved. In 1814 he wrote a letter to John Morgan, a moving and heartfelt plea about his addiction in which he states, *What crime is there scarcely which has not been included in or followed from the one guilt of taking opium?* He realised that he could not conquer the addiction himself and in a letter to his friend Wade in 1814 wrote that one possible solution could be subjecting himself to be in effect held in forcible confinement and that *all in the house were forbidden to fetch anything but by the Doctor's order.* I think one thing that we have to acknowledge here is that his friends, such as Southey, probably through ignorance, signally failed to help him.'

'Are you saying we should excuse his drug-taking?' someone asked.

'I think what I'm saying is that we should understand his addiction and that, those who were close at hand, could definitely have done more to help.'

'It's the same problem now,' another said.

Desdemona unexpectedly had returned and began

participating in the conversation as though she had not left.

'I think you're all ignoring the elephant in the room,' she said.

'Which is?' the Prof said.

'The question I would like to ask is, what would Coleridge have achieved if he was not using opium. May there not be a case for saying that his use of opium stimulated him to write some of his greatest poems?'

'That's a good question – a provocative question.' There was nervous laughter, but I think from the Prof's point of view, he was glad she had returned. 'But a good question nevertheless, and it may be impossible to give a definitive answer. But perhaps we can give it a go. We could start by assessing the extent of his opium taking and look at the extent of his achievements. The last of these is important as some commentators have suggested that his poetry writing began and ended at Nether Stowey and, of course, we must recognise that we cannot judge Coleridge from his poetry alone. His achievement in other fields of writing should not be underestimated.

'Firstly, we need to recognise that Coleridge undoubtedly had acquired a habit of regularly taking opium by the time, as I have said, he attended Cambridge University. He had bouts of crippling anxiety followed by periods of intense excitement. His time at university also included bouts of heavy drinking and promiscuity. We also know that in 1796, the recently married Coleridge wrote a letter to a friend stating the pressures he was under, including the pregnancy of his wife, Sarah. In the letter he stated that he had been forced to take opium every day. So, we know that he was taking opium at a much earlier period than was formerly thought.

'We also need to recognise that Coleridge was a patient of Doctor Beddoes. The importance of this is that Beddoes was a follower of Dr John Brown of Edinburgh who maintained that opium was a proper means of gaining stimulation and health. Beddoes also employed the services of the inventor Humphry Davy to help him in the use of gases to cure some of his patients' ailments. Thomas Wedgwood who, along with Josiah Wedgwood was his benefactor, was also a member if this opium circle. We know that Coleridge tried nitrous oxide and other stimulants. And, of course, Coleridge was also a friend of Thomas de Quincey who wrote *Confessions of an English Opium Eater* where he encouraged the use of opium. In fact, it could be argued that opium was the go-to stimulant of the Romantic poets. Shelley, Keats and Byron were all opium users as were Elizabeth Barrett Browning, Dorothy Wordsworth and George Eliot.

'So, Coleridge's' use of opium was not unusual, but I think we have to conclude that Coleridge's use of opium, perhaps unlike some of his friends' use of opium, did amount to a genuine addiction. We also know from his letters, as I have said, that Coleridge was aware of this – and made several attempts to moderate his use or give it up.

'Step in Doctor Gilman, suggested by a fellow doctor, Adams, who was treating Coleridge when he returned to London in March 1816 and his health had crashed. Gilman took Coleridge into his home in Highgate and, though he was not able to cure Coleridge of his addiction, he was able to moderate it.

'The next question then is, the one that you have asked: is there any way in which the use of opium contributed to his writing of poetry. The two example most quoted with respect to this are "Kubla Khan" and "The Rime of the Ancient Mariner". The answer is probably, yes to a degree, in the same way that perhaps in another era the Beatles were inspired by LSD to write "Lucy in the Sky with Diamonds" and other of their songs. We also know that in both cases their talents did not absolutely rely on this. Despite, for example, that Coleridge insisted that "Kubla Khan" was written in a drug induced reverie, he was an inveterate reviser of works and that did not depend exclusively on them being written under the hallucinatory effects of opium use.

'So, let's look at it from the other side. Did his overuse of opium harm his further output of poetry? Again, the answer is probably yes. He wrote in a letter to William Godwin in March 1801, *The poet is dead in me*. He wrote a valedictory poem, "Dejection, an Ode". The irony, of course, is that this is a poem where we find him at the peak of his poetical powers.'

The Prof paused.

'I guess that does not answer your question fully, Desdemona.'

'It doesn't completely, but I appreciate you have tried to give an answer. We could also talk about the fact that the use of hallucinogens is now increasingly considered as a *bona fide* treatment for PSD and other forms of depression and anxiety. There is a case for arguing that it may have helped Coleridge to some degree with the trauma he suffered as a child. It may have been better if he had cut out his alcohol consumption as that causes a far greater number of deaths.'

There was more laughter here – though I think Desdemona was being deadly serious.

'I don't claim to have widespread knowledge of these drugs but from the research I have done in this matter, I stand by what I say. I also want to return to the point about Coleridge's output after he left Nether Stowey. Too many people, I feel, have taken Coleridge at his own word about the death of his poetry. There were more poems that came later. He was self-deprecating, calling them *copy verses*. Yet in one case he would say *in sentiment and music of verse …it is equal to anything I wrote*. Examples of this are "Youth and Age", "Work Without Hope", "Limbo", "Ne Plus Ultra" and "Love, Hope and Patience in Education". He may never have scaled the heights of his great poems written in Nether Stowey, but these are seriously accomplished poems.

'The other important question, I think, is what else, apart from poetry, did he achieve in the years after he left Nether Stowey? And the answer is quite a damned lot.'

He went on describe Coleridge's achievements following his time in The Quantocks: his journey to Germany with the Wordsworths where he learnt the German language and studied German literature and philosophy attending Gottingen University (a key part of his intellectual development that had a lasting impact on English Romanticism); the *Biographia Literaria* which he wrote on his return from Germany in 1799, a literary autobiography which also discussed the theory of poetry and his own philosophy; the series of lectures on the principles of poetry and other subjects at The Royal Institution between 1808-1814 (his lectures on Shakespeare had been ground-breaking and were influential in a general revival of interest in Shakespeare's work); *The Friend Magazine* based on weekly essays from 1 June 1809 to 15 March 1810; the publication of "Christabel" in 1816 along with "Kubla Khan" and "The Pains of Sleep" and the following year his collected poems, *Sibylline Leaves*; the occasional verse and philosophical lectures which he gave in 1818; a collection of moral and physical aphorisms published in "Aids to Reflection" in 1825; a meditation on political inspiration in *The Statemen's Manual* published in 1816; *The Constitution of Church and State* which appeared in 1830, and *Confessions of Inquiring Spirit* which was published after his death in 1840. He was also still working at his death on a comprehensive philosophical work, never finished, part of which was published as *Hints Towards the Formation of a More Comprehensive Theory of Life*.

The Prof then came to his conclusion.

'So, to answer the general question. Yes, his addiction no doubt did affect the extent and quality of his output but to say his important work was done by the time he left Nether Stowey, I think, is wrong. Even if we ignore his later poetry, which as I have said, does in any case have some serious merit, his later philosophical and metaphysical writings and literary criticism were enormously important and influence us even today. In conclusion, I would say that he achieved an awful lot despite his addiction but there is no doubt he may have achieved more had he not had it.'

There was time for a few more quick questions.

'Wow,' I said afterwards, 'we're really covering the ground here.'

'And you can see how over 200 years later passions are still roused,' said Jonahan.

During the break a buffet was served. There was a lot of chatter but it was difficult to hear what was being said so I contented myself with taking a stroll outside and sitting on some steps to admire the view and take in some air before we all assembled again for the musical version of "The Rime of The Ancient Mariner".

Jonathan stood up and spoke.

'Before the next event, we do have a special announcement to make about a new acquisition to our Coleridge collection, and that is none other than an original of the 1800 edition of *Lyrical Ballads*.'

There were sounds of appreciation.

'Yes, I know, it is a great addition to the collection. And it has been donated by booksellers Ex Libris. The bookshop owner, Elliot Todd, was gifted the book and felt that it was more appropriate in our hands. He has made a visit to check that we are a *bona fide* organisation,' there was some laughter at this point, 'and to present the book to us. It's on display in this splendid cabinet. I'm afraid because of its rarity it is not available to pick up and read but we do plan in the future a session where can examine the book in more detail under the watchful eye of the library curator. But for now, I would like to introduce you to our benefactor Elliot Todd from Ex Libris.'

There was generous applause.

'Thank you, Jonathan,' I said.'I don't intend saying anything much except that having attended your excellent sessions on Thomas Poole and Coleridge and having been in the company of Jonathan and Dora, I can see that in donating the book to the Coleridge Society Ex Libris has made exactly the correct decision.'

The moment in my nightmare when Cantalbrini confronted me and fired a shot at me came back into my mind. I sneaked a quick look around the audience. There were smiling faces and no hint of an interruption. I made a cough to excuse my hesitation and continued.

'I have witnessed your expertise, enthusiasm and, indeed passion, for all things Coleridge. And it has rubbed off on me. I, of course, knew something of Coleridge and his poetry before I came here, but now I know so much more and, like you are, I am entranced by this extraordinary individual and those who came into contact with him.'

There was generous applause. Jonathan spoke again.

'Then it only remains for me to thank you, and, because of your generosity, I have something to give you in return.'

He handed me an envelope.

'What's this?'

'Why don't you open it?'

My hands were a little shaky but eventually I was able to extract the paper inside.

'An honorary membership for life of the Coleridge Society. That's fantastic.'

'We understand that you won't be able to make all the meetings or events, but it would be great if you could come and see us now and again.'

'Thank you, I will.'

I shook hands with Jonathan and left the stage, once more to applause.

We then went straight into a recording of a musical version of "The Rime of the Ancient" with music by Howard Skempton and sung by Roderick Williams.

The recording took about half-an-hour, after which we dispersed, with much chatter and excitement. I felt pleased to be involved and said as much to Jonathan and Dora in the car on the way to their home. They were in a playful mood.

'I have learnt so much about Coleridge and the people he knew, and about this part of Somerset. I feel a different person from when I first came here.'

'Well, in a way you are,' said Jonathan.

'Like Odysseus in *The Odyssey*,' said Dora.

'Your journey has been The Coleridge Way,' said Jonathan.

'Though wasn't Odysseus's journey ten years? Mine was only a few days.'

They ignored this small detail.

'There are other parallels too,' said Dora. 'You have narrowly escaped harm like Odysseus when he was shipwrecked and clung to a fig tree.'

That's an interesting one,' I said. 'I clung to a bush to break my fall at the cliff edge.'

'Precisely,' said Jonathan. 'But I'm not sure if we should be reminding Elliot about that.'

'You've been held captive in our house having angered the sea god at Lynmouth,' said Dora, ignoring Jonathan's words of caution.

'And, of course, it has been a journey of the mind and the accumulation of wisdom,' added Jonathan, possibly trying to move away from references to the danger I had been in on the cliff edge at Lynton.

'Not sure about that last one.'

'Oh yes, no doubt about it; your knowledge and understanding of Coleridge has made you much wiser, I'm sure,' said Dora.

'Of course, we would say that as members of the Coleridge Society,' said Jonathan. 'Now all you have to do is return to your bookshop and slay the suitors to your Penelope.'

Of, course, I thought immediately of Esther and then, immediately afterwards wondered, if she had other suitors.

'Not sure if I'm quite ready for that.'

'Well, in any case, you could say you have experienced a kind of *Somerset Odyssey*.'

'OK, I will accept that, and I feel all the better for it. It's funny you should say that as I was having a chat with my friend Esther the other day and we made a comparison with *The Odyssey* and Coleridge's life as a kind of metaphorical odyssey.

'I think you're onto something there, Elliot,' said Dora. 'His life involved significant journeys at home and abroad and, of course journeys of the mind and spirit as well his struggles with addiction and personal relationships.'

They were performing like a double act. Jonathan backed her up.

'Interesting observation. We'll have to get you to talk to the Prof about that. Might ask you to do an article in our bulletin.'

It had been a long day, and, having eaten already at the buffet, we all agreed on an early night. I excused myself and went straight up to bed. I found sleep almost straight away, unlike the evening before.

19

The following day there was to be a reading of "Kubla Kahn" followed by an examination of the text by the Prof with a chance to make comments. Desdemona was to read the text.

'It will be quite something,' said Dora. 'She puts everything into it.'

But there was a problem. Desdemona was not there. Alice made an announcement.

'We're just waiting for our reader. Looks like she's running late.'

Phone calls were made. A plan was hatched. Someone was going to go around to her house. She was only a ten-minute walk away.

Alice came over to Dora.

'Dora, do you think you would mind? The Prof would do it himself but I think it may be better to have someone else so he can concentrate on what he's going to say.'

'Yes, of course.'

Jonathan squeezed her hand and wished her good luck.

Dora began reading the lines that we had 'walked' the day before when we followed the lines of stones in the park at Ottery St Mary. She did a very good job reading her lines out loud and clear with good expression.

'Beautifully read,' said the Prof. 'Now let's examine some of the lines.'

Like the previous sessions, it was very informative with Coleridge members making significant contributions during the question and answer session.

Of course, the question of the person from Porlock came up, the visitor on business who had, supposedly interrupted Coleridge in the middle of writing the complete poem that was, he claimed, in his head following an opium inspired dream. What we were left with, according to Coleridge, was a shortened version of what was intended. But the professor disagreed; the poem was not, in his opinion, a fragment but stands up as a complete poem in its own right, once again putting into question the veracity of the theory about the person from Porlock.

Just as we were finishing our session, a tearful Desdemona turned up. She sat at the back but only stayed a few minutes and left again before the end.

'I'm afraid I didn't get a chance to speak to her,' said Dora after the event had finished. 'I guess her son still hasn't come back or they have had another argument. I'll try ringing her.'

The concluding event of the Coleridge weekend was a meal at the ancient Ship Inn at Porlock Weir.

I sat between Jonathan and Dora. There were about twenty of us and there was almost constant chatter. It was not very long before the words Coleridge or Wordsworth or Sarah were mentioned, but also, I noticed the name of Desdemona coming up a few times.

'I've so enjoyed my visit,' I said to Jonathan and Dora, 'and I really value my membership. I will try and return next year.'

'You would be very welcome.'

There was an empty space at the table.

'No Desdemona again,' someone said.

A lady I did not recognise entered the pub, approached Jonathan and whispered in his ear.

'Oh, that's too sad,' I heard him say.

'What is it, Jonathan?' asked Dora.

'It's Desdemona; Cassio has been found in a coma. They think it may be an overdose.'

The atmosphere became more sombre. Desdemona's place setting was taken away. There was much heartfelt talk in hushed tones, often involving Jonathan and Dora.

'The poor woman,' said Dora.

'So sad,' said Jonathan.

'We all know Desdemona dabbled in drugs but as far as we knew, Cassio didn't.'

'It may be pills, not drugs.'

'It maybe an attempted suicide.'

The assembled company had lost some of its spark. We all decided on an early departure, but not before a speech by the Prof in which we drank to the good health of STC and Sarah.

I awoke early the next morning to hear Dora and Jonathan talking.

Dora was very animated. I went down in my pyjamas to check that everything was OK.

Dora was crying and Jonathan had his arm around her shoulder.

'Desdemona was inconsolable. She blames herself. You see, Cassio had a stutter – especially when he got stressed. She persuaded him to have some cocaine, and it worked. His stuttering went. Then he became addicted. His personality changed and he came more aggressive. He pushed her and left her with a bruise on her arm. He would never have done that before. He was the gentlest of people. Then some money went missing. He didn't have enough for cocaine, she thinks. That's when he bought some ketamine – apparently its much cheaper - and the overdose happened. It's all so sad.'

20

Travelling back on the train the next day I felt a strange mixture of emotions; a sense of well-being mixed with occasional anxiety. I had enjoyed learning more about the fascinating life of Coleridge and meeting with the knowledgeable and diverse Coleridge Society membership and, especially meeting and staying with Jonathan and his wife, while the walk, despite the incident at the cliff edge, had been, for the most part, a joyful experience.

Looking in the mirror on the morning before my departure I thought I noticed a slight thinning around the stomach area. At the same time, much as I tried to put it out of my mind, the tragic circumstances of Desdemona's son kept entering my head at unexpected moments.

The police had contacted me to say that at this stage they could not pursue a formal investigation regarding the attack on me due to the lack of evidence. No further action could be taken without credible proof. They were at pains to say that this did not mean that they did not believe me. The incident was recorded and supported by my statement, which might be valuable if further information came to light. In any case, I supposed they probably now had more urgent business to attend to with the plight of Michael Cassio. There was no need for me to remain in the area. They had my contact details and would contact me if any further evidence came to light.

There was something, though, that was bothering me. I had not yet told Esther about my attack. In the past year or so she had been the first person I confided in. I knew I would have to tell her and had intended doing so before I returned, but the more time elapsed, the more difficult I found it to contemplate the moment when I would.

I did not have a book to read (having had mine stolen) so resorted to my phone. I checked for any mentions of Ex

Libris on Facebook. Esther had put up some new titles which could be ordered from our bookshop. Dora's name and a few others from the Coleridge Society came up as possible friend suggestions. I liked the idea of learning about the latest goings on of Coleridge Society members so asked them to be my friends.

I sent a message to Esther saying that I had made the train OK and that I looked forward to seeing her later. My carriage was virtually empty at that early stage of the journey, so I decided to risk a call to Laura. She answered right away.'

'Ciao,' I said.

'Oh, hi Elliot. What news do you have for me?'

I told her about being pushed off the cliff and my rucksack being stolen.

'Oh, my goodness. How awful for you?'

'I don't know if you think this is crazy, but I wondered if it was anything to do with Cantalbrini?'

'Hm, yes well, I don't know but anything is possible. I'm not sure if Cantalbrini is allowed to travel abroad at the moment with the ongoing investigation, but I wonder?'

'Would it be worth his while, in any case? I guess, compared to some of the things he sells, *Lyrical Ballads* would be considered of relatively modest value.'

'With people like Cantalbrini it's not just about value. It's also about things like honour and betrayal.'

'Yes, I had thought that.'

'Let me do a bit of research and I will get back to you.'

I arrived back at the bookshop in the early afternoon. Aggie had just worked the morning as she was looking after grandchildren in the afternoon, so I knew Esther would be on her own. She gave me a quick hug.

'Good to see you,' she said.

'Yes, and you. Have you had any lunch?'

'I was trying to sneak a sandwich behind the counter, but it's been a bit busy.'

'I've had something on the train. Why don't you take a break now?'

There was much to catch up on over the rest of the day, the

penalty of going away on a break when you own your own business. There were urgent bills to pay, orders to process, author talk enquiries to follow up and, of course, and most important of all, customers to serve. There was really very little time to chat about the rest of my visit to the West Country until we closed the door on the shop. However, it was also yoga night for Esther which meant she had to leave promptly.

'Sorry we can't chat. Perhaps after my yoga?' she said as she was leaving.

'Curry?' I suggested.

'At the Gurkha?'

'Yes, I'll book a table. 8.30, OK?'

'Yes.'

And with that, she was gone.

I rang my mother as soon as I arrived home, aware that I had not been in touch for a while. There was no reply so I left a message that I was just catching up, that I was out that evening but was free after that.

'You haven't told me much about what happened after I left you,' said Esther taking a swig of her Cobra beer once we had ordered our food after meeting up at the restaurant.

'Well, there's quite a bit to tell, but first of all, I have to say, Jonathan and his wife were so nice.'

I told her about my trip to Ottery St Mary, the events and the presentation and the news that Michael Cassio was in a coma.

Esther went to the loo and when she returned there was, for a moment, an awkward silence. I wanted to tell her about the cliff incident. I took a swig of my own pint and hesitated, wondering how much to explain, whether to explain at all.

'I know you Elliot Todd, you're not being yourself.' She put her hand to her forehead. 'There's something else you're not telling me.'

'I...there is but I find it difficult...'

'Was it something to do with the book? Was it not what they expected?'

'No, not that. They were really pleased.'

'You didn't have an affair with the club secretary?'

'No, not the club secretary... or anyone else.'

Then I told her about the man grabbing my rucksack and pushing me so that I fell off the edge of the cliff.

She was shocked, as I had expected she would be.

'Oh Elliot, this break was supposed to be for you to get over things, not for things to be made worse.'

She took my hands towards her, which I only at that moment realised I had been clenching together on the table as I was speaking.

'I'm so glad you're all right. How on earth did you survive?'

'More by luck than judgement – and desperation. I guess I was afraid of dying.'

I was trying to be nonchalant, but I had been terrified, and it had shaken me.

'We'll get over this, don't worry.'

The waiter came over at that moment and brought some poppadoms and pickles.

When he had gone, I went on to explain about the police and how it remained under review to see if any further evidence came forward.

We explored the motive over chicken tikka.

'It has to be something to do with Cantalbrini doesn't it?' said Esther. 'I feel a fool about the Facebook thing. It was obviously an invitation for him to know that you would taking the *Lyrical Ballads* down to the West Country – even though you didn't.'

'You mustn't blame yourself. I'm a bit surprised that they didn't think I may have couriered it, in any case.'

'Well, sending by courier is not always infallible nowadays. Cantalbrini is probably the sort of person who would rather deliver something in person to take the risk away from it getting lost or stolen and perhaps he thought you felt the same way.'

'I suppose that's true. Anyway, I did tell the police about it. They were going to make enquires with the Rome police. I gave them Alessandro's name, though I got the impression the police in Lynton were a bit sceptical about that theory.'

'Best to tell them everything you know. But, if not that, what else could it be?'

'I suppose whoever it was could've just been after money and credit cards. Or he might just have been unhinged. Oh, and I also rang Laura to see what she thought.'

'What *did* she think?'

'She didn't really give anything away but said she would make some enquiries. I get the feeling that she's more likely to believe it is something to do with Cantalbrini than our own police.'

'I guess that's due to the nature of the business she's in and, for her, thefts of books are commonplace. Do you know if he was Italian… did he say anything?'

'From his looks he could easily have been Italian, but he didn't say a word. But then, people have sometimes mistaken me for Italian – until I open my mouth. I did see him earlier though, so I think he must have been following me.'

I explained about my sighting of him on the Cliff Railway in Lynmouth.

'Well, I guess that means it's more likely he is one of Cantalbrini's cohorts and that it was a pre-meditated plan. But why would it mean so much to Cantalbrini?'

'Laura thinks that the book was to buy my silence about the death of Mr Abruzzio. I'd already told the police in any case. I've never been very good at picking up on social codes.'

'Yes, I can confirm that. That's probably why you've never married.'

It was a pointed remark, though my mind was on other things at that moment.

'I should never have taken the book when he gave it to me. I should've been braver then. I was just thinking about getting out of his flat. He was unnerving me.'

'You can't blame yourself. And you mustn't let this define you. It's a freak occurrence and we will get over it together. It's like after I was attacked during that awful business with the First Folio. You stood by me then and I will stand by you now.'

'That does make me feel better,' I said.

She still had a small scar on her face. For me it did not detract from her beauty. She squeezed my hand. We ordered dessert. The waiter came over.

'Is everything OK?'

'Yes, lovely, thank you,' we both said.

How English we both were.

'But we both need another beer,' added Esther. 'God, we really do,' said Esther after the waiter had gone.

I felt so much happier after having told Esther. Her emotional support made me feel more able to cope with the situation and I slept well that night. The next day I spent a pleasant time catching up with Aggie at the bookshop. I reminded her that we would be visiting Simon at the weekend for an informal afternoon tea and discussion of his new environmental project.

'I'm not sure what advice I can give but I do enjoy a good cup of tea and a sandwich,' said Aggie.

'That's one thing I can assure you; it will be the best tea, and the sandwiches will be first class.'

A visit to Simon and Miriam had always been a pleasurable experience for me, especially where food and drink were concerned.

'Yes, I have heard about your visits and your tendency to overindulge. Would you like me to drive by the way? Then you and Esther can have a drink.'

'Would you Aggie? That's really sweet of you.'

I didn't hear back from my mother on the Wednesday evening so called again and left a message on Thursday evening.

21

The next morning, I had a phone call from Laura.

'Ciao.'

'Ciao.'

'I have been doing some research and its quite interesting. Cantalbrini has a son, Georgio, who lives in the UK.'

'So, it could have been him that attacked me, on instructions from his father.'

'I think it's a distinct possibility.'

'So where do we go from here?'

'Well, obviously, we need proof, and in order to get that, we need a photo and to locate him and ask him a few questions. We think it's best to try to find him before talking to Cantalbrini, otherwise he might warn him off. We'll liaise with the British police and take it from there.'

'That all sounds very good. Is there anything I need to do?'

'Just make sure your memory bank is in good order.'

Aggie, as arranged, picked me up in her Citroën Dyane. Then we travelled on to Esther's cottage and arrived at Simon's just after midday.

We gathered, in brilliant late August sunshine, in the courtyard area at the front of the house, admiring the mix of flowers in pots and hanging baskets before Simon emerged.

'I was thinking,' I said to Simon, as we made our way around the house to the gardens, 'I think you said you have five acres. That's perfect, the same as one of the examples in John Seymour's book.'

'Yes, that had occurred to me too.'

I was surprised by how much had already changed since my last visit. A considerable area, which was once part of an extensive lawn, was now bare soil. Part of me regretted the absence of the soft green swathe of lawn. I wondered if this was how it was during wartime during the dig for victory campaign. Many comparisons have been made between the climate emergency and the second world war, with some claiming that we should treat our climate problems as though we were on a war footing.

'I thought it was best to have the vegetable patch close to the house,' Simon expounded. 'The idea is that we can nip out and pick up a lettuce or bunch of potatoes as we need it.'

When he said *we* I suspected he meant Miriam.

'The first thing I would like to do is decide on where to put the chicken run.'

We walked around the gabled end of the house into a large open space punctuated by trees, and with a pond. We stood in our motley group on the terrace and looked to the four corners of the garden.

'What a beautiful garden!' exclaimed Aggie.

We all murmured our agreement, but Simon's mind was bent on more practical things.

'So, where would you think I should site the chicken run?' he inquired of Esther.

Esther, as ever, was not backward in coming forward.

'Well, of course, you're extremely lucky to have all this space to choose from.'

'Granted.'

'When I put mine in, I didn't have so much choice, but I remember I was told not to have the coop in direct sunlight but that a combination of sun and shade is good.'

'That seems sensible.'

'So, a place partly shaded by a tree would be good.'

She walked in the direction of a well-established tree. We all followed.

'What about this lovely old Sycamore?'

'Yes, why not? What about the ground?'

'Ideally, the ground should be nice and even. Not rocky, so the chickens can scratch around but not somewhere that can be waterlogged. I made that mistake initially and had to move it across a bit to a drier area.'

'That's all eminently sensible. I'm so glad we are having this conversation.'

'But, of course, one of the most important things is to

125

keep the fox away,' she continued. 'So, you need to make it predator proof. You want them to have plenty of room to run around but you need to put up fencing so that foxes can't get through.'

'Have you lost any to the fox?'

'Not yet, but I feel you can never relax or become complacent.'

'Of course.'

'One of the biggest things to consider, of course, is which breed of chickens you are going to have and how many.'

'Yes, what do you suggest?'

'Well, you could try to get some battery farm chickens and rescue them from their previously wretched existence. They may not, though, lay as many eggs as you want. And then it's a case of how attractive you want them to look.'

'Attractive?'

'Yes, well you know, one of the reasons people keep chickens is that they can look very nice.'

'It's true,' I said. 'Esther has some of the most attractive chickens around.'

'Why, Mr Todd, flattery will get you everywhere.' She used an American accent and fluttered her eyelashes at me to general laughter.

'For example, a Silkie is known for its gentle nature and is attractive to look at', she continued. 'They make great companions but do not lay a lot of eggs.'

'I must admit, I'd never thought of it as a beauty contest,' laughed Simon. 'I don't suppose you would help me choose them?'

'I'd be delighted.'

'What's your price?'

'A good lunch.'

'Coming right up.'

We walked further, past the sycamore tree and the position of the imagined hen house and into an area of patchy ground containing a few small trees and shrubs.

'And this is where I would like my orchard. Aggie, do you have any views?'

'I have one or two trees at home, but I have to say it's not really my area of expertise.'

'I know who can help, though,' said Esther. 'My friend Chloe.'

'Yes, of course,' I said. 'I'd forgotten about her – her expertise, I mean - with growing apples.'

We had visited Chloe earlier in the year when returning from the London Book Fair.

'Chloe,' continued Esther, 'has a variety of apple trees that give fruit from July to the beginning of November.

'Really, I thought they were just an autumn thing,' said Simon.

'You know, she could do with a break. I don't know if I should mention this, but her husband works away on an oil rig. She might agree to come and stay – if she can drag herself away from her art.'

'She's a brilliant artist,' I confirmed.

'Seriously, if she agreed to come and give some advice I would compensate her for her time. It would only be fair.'

'I thought you might object as her husband works with oil.'

'Well, yes, we must keep it in the ground, no doubt about that – but I can't blame her for her husband's work.'

A gong went. I knew that sound well.

'Dinner is about to be served,' I said.

'Yes, Miriam doesn't like it if we're late. Perhaps we can talk about vegetables over lunch, Aggie.'

'You mean we can talk about vegetables over the vegetables?'

'Quite right!'

I was expecting that we would eat in the dining room but, as we approached the front of the house, I saw a table outside already laid with cutlery and wine glasses glistening in the sun, and beneath, a red and white check tablecloth.

'Are there seating arrangements? I can't see any white cards,' said Esther.

'Well, I think, given that they are the ones with the knowledge, that Esther and Aggie should be sitting either side of me,' said Simon.

'You know how to put a fellow down,' I said.

He strode to the end of the table, sat down and gestured

towards Esther and Aggie and the two seats either side of him.

'Well, that's lucky for me,' I said, 'I'll have the benefit of Miriam's company.'

I said this as Miriam approached with a tray of piping hot potatoes and veg. I walked back with her towards the kitchen to help bring out the rest of the dinner.

'Are you OK with all this?' I said to Miriam. 'I get the impression that it may have been foisted on you.'

'Yes, and yes. It was foisted on me, as you know these things usually are by Simon. But I'm perfectly happy with it, and I agree with his reasons for doing it. Do you think he's being too crazy, or do you think all this ecology stuff is a good idea?'

'Well, yes and yes. He's undoubtedly on the edge of madness as he has proved several times with his various projects, but yes, I agree he is right to take it seriously, especially as I benefit from it.'

'In what way?'

'He's allowing me to store books in his barn, which is going to be covered with solar panels, a key part of his project, he said - and he has already bought books on the subject. I suspect there will be many more purchases. So, really, I benefit twice.'

'Can you carry that out for me?'

She put into my hands a giant pot.

Simon appeared.

'Just one thing missing, a couple of bottles of plonk.'

'Don't forget a soft drink for Aggie,' Miriam reminded him.

As we loaded up our plates with the delicious food, Simon busied himself with the wine and eventually extracted a cork accompanied by a satisfying pop.

'I love that sound,' said Esther.

'It's a nice bottle of Graves. Just right for such an important occasion,' said Simon.

'Why did I decide to drive?' said Aggie.

'There's some delicious sparkling apple juice,' said Miriam.

'No, I'm not missing out, give me a half glass and we can take the back roads home.'

'There aren't any other sorts of roads around here,' I reminded her.

'So nice to have you all here together,' said Miriam. 'Elliot, can you take the lid off that pot you just brought in?'

As I lifted the lid, a wonderful smell wafted in my direction.

'Ah, chicken tagine, I think,' said Esther.

Within the pot, as well as the chicken, was a wonderful array of Mediterranean style vegetables.

'There's also a quiche for those who want a vegetarian option,' said Miriam.

There was a respectful silence, punctuated by appreciative grunts, while we all tucked into the delicious food.

'There's one other thing that I wanted to mention in addition to the things I have talked about,' Simon said at last. 'This is more of a pet project. I can't really claim that it has the same green credentials – though I want it to be organic as far as possible.'

'I know what's coming,' said Miriam.

'What is it? Do explain,' said Esther.

'Oh, yes, I think I know too,' I said.

I looked conspiratorially in Miriam's direction.

'A vineyard!'

'Maybe a vineyard is too grand a term but certainly a few vines.'

'Well, you have to,' I said reaching for a glass of the perfectly chilled Graves.

'How exciting,' said Aggie.

'Can we help with that?' asked Esther. 'We don't know anything about growing grapes, of course, but we can be your tasting experts. And we don't charge for our expertise, do we Elliot?'

'No, not at all. A couple of bottles of Château de Bonneville from your latest vintage will suffice.'

'Well, that's settled then.'

The tagine was finished but I knew from experience that this was not the end of the feast, and we were soon treated to jam roly-poly and custard.

'I'm in heaven,' said Aggie. 'Just like my mother used to make.'

'I'm so pleased you're enjoying it Aggie, but I forgot to ask you about the vegetables over the vegetables,' said Simon.

'Yes, well, I'm flattered that you asked me over to give advice, Simon, I really am. The problem is though, I think I'm here under false pretences. I do grow vegetables and have quite a bit of success...'

'Everything you give me is always the best quality and scrumptious,' I confirmed.

'The truth of the matter is there's not much method to how I grow things. To be honest, I'm not sure what I do. It just happens.'

'*Benign neglect* is a phrase I often hear you use,' said Esther.

'Isn't that the phrase she applied to bringing up her children as well?' I added.

Aggie ignored me.

'Yes, well, it's sometimes true that too much watering can sometimes be as bad as not enough watering.'

'What if you came here and applied some of your benign neglect? I would pay you for your time, of course.'

I pretended outrage.

'Simon, you're poaching my most senior employee!'

'Sorry.'

'No, you're not,' said Aggie. 'He does give me the odd day off now and again and I do love working in the garden in any case. Anyway, when he says most senior employee, he just means that I'm old. You notice he didn't say best.'

'Ouch!' said Simon.

'Anyway, you can't make her stay,' said Esther to me. 'She's free to go and work wherever she likes. We're not your indentured slaves, even though you treat us as though we are.'

'Oh, dear, employee relations not too good at the moment?' chipped in Simon.

'But you don't want Aggie to leave, do you?' I said to Esther.

'Of course not.'

'Nobody's talking about leaving,' said Aggie. 'I'm quite capable of, you know of...'

'Mixing it up,' said Esther.

'Muddling through,' I said.

'Multi-tasking,' said Miriam.

'That's exactly the phrase I was looking for, thank you Miriam.'

22

I was working with Aggie the following day but as I walked to work the next morning, there was something in the back of my mind, something not quite right that was bothering me, and I could not quite call it to mind.

I unlocked the door, switched off the alarm and put an A-board out advertising a forthcoming talk. Aggie turned up as I was doing so.

'Here's some courgettes for you.'

'Oh, thank you, Aggie.' I thought about the other three I still had sitting in the fridge. *Time to make that ratatouille*, I thought.

That reminded me of the conversation with Simon at the previous day's lunch.

'When are you going to see Simon about your new role as vegetable ambassador?'

'Next Thursday.'

And then I remembered.

'Ah, I know what it is!'

'Know what what is? You're not making sense, Elliot.'

'There was something bothering me. Now I know what it is. My mother didn't ring on Friday. I haven't spoken to her for so long now.'

'Oh, well you can give her a ring now.'

'But it's so unusual for her not to ring. On the rare occasions I'm not there she always leaves a message.'

Aggie was looking at me, no doubt wondering what all the fuss was about.

'I'll ring her now.'

I went upstairs to ring her from the office on the shop phone so that we had some privacy. There was no answer. I would try her later I told Aggie.

'Wasn't she going somewhere – to look at some cult thing, I remember you saying?'

'She was, though I don't know why it would stop her ringing. But you're right, she's probably busy. It's all part of her project. She may have a deadline or something.'

I tried not to worry. But I failed to be able to get through to her after further attempts that evening.

I rang Esther. She often knew more about what my mother was doing than I did. They sometimes had secret conversations that were inadvertently revealed at a later date. Esther, as usual, sought to reassure me.

'It's a little unusual but it's probably something to do with her project. Wasn't she travelling down to the West Country again? What did she say to you the last time you spoke?'

'Aggie said something similar. I don't think she gave me a specific date for her trip, but I can't really remember. Sometimes our conversations go all over the place.'

'You mean you switch off and are not really listening?'

I changed the subject.

'How's your dad?'

'He's fine. Busy as ever. He keeps asking about you. Says he'd like to meet you.'

'Well, if the opportunity arises.'

It was always difficult for Esther and me to be away together, as her recent short time away visiting me in Somerset had proved.

Esther returned to the idea of my mother not getting in touch.

'What about that friend of Elizabeth's a couple of doors down?'

'Belinda. Yes, that's a thought. I don't think I have a number, though.'

'It's OK, I think I have.'

'Why have you got her number rather than me? OK, don't answer that.'

I was able to get through to Belinda on the first attempt.

'Your mum's fine, as far as I know. In fact, she's been in very good form - and quite excited. She's gone away on some course thing. I've got it somewhere.'

The phone went dead for a while.

'Here it is, it's near Glastonbury. It's called The Beacon. They do Bed and Breakfast, it seems.'

'Thanks, Belinda. I'm sorry to worry you. I'm sure it's all fine.'

'Perhaps the signal is very poor down there with all those hills.'

'Yes, you're probably right.'

I looked up The Beacon. Belinda was right. I was sceptical when she said it, but they did do Bed and Breakfast. Why on earth didn't my mother mention it to me, though? Unless she was meeting someone special? (she nearly got married to a technician at the local university the previous year) and did not want me to know about it.

When I looked a bit further on the website there was a section under Life Coaching Courses. I clicked on the link. There were a variety of options which claimed to transform your life and empower you. You could book in for a course and the Bed and Breakfast facility together. That was entirely logical. If you were to run courses, you may as well offer accommodation as well. It made good business sense.

I rang Esther.

'So, it seems like she has booked into the Bed and Breakfast...'

'And, I guess, must be attending one of the courses.'

I heard the tapping of a keyboard.

'It says it's life-coaching. Professional development. Is that going to be a cult?'

'Obviously, they don't announce themselves as cults.'

'Well, maybe she is not going because she thinks it's a cult but because she really does want some life-coaching.'

'Really. Elizabeth, life coaching?'

'Maybe not. Except you know, I know it was a few years ago now, but she may be still dealing with the death of your father - and there was that chap she nearly married.'

'But found him too boring, thank God!'

'But they were close for a while. You shouldn't belittle a relationship just because it doesn't fit into your scheme of things. He might have been boring but probably had other good qualities. Stability and security are an underrated quality.' I wondered if this was an oblique reference to myself. 'She is probably wondering where she goes with her life.'

'I'll leave a message at reception at the Bed and Breakfast

and ask her to ring me. Even if her phone is out of order there must be a payphone or phone in the B and B she can use.'

'Good idea.'

I got through to The Beacon on the second attempt. I made it clear it was not urgent but asked if she could contact me as soon as possible. The receptionist said that she would leave the details but that my mother was involved in a heavy programme of work where they were encouraged to isolate themselves from the outside world, that this included handing in your phone, and that she may not be able to get back to me immediately.

I reported back to Esther.

'I wonder what a heavy work programme entails?' she said.

I did not hear from my mother that morning or in the afternoon.

'She'll probably ring in the evening,' Esther said to me before I left the shop for home, 'when her work programme for the day has finished.'

I went home and cooked myself an omelet. I was trying to finish up some of the eggs that Esther had recently passed on to me. Her chickens were in a particularly productive period. My egg consumption had quadrupled since Esther had started working at the shop. When I raised the problem of cholesterol in eggs, she assured me that this was a different kind from the one that had got a bad name. Eggs produced a healthy type of cholesterol, she had explained to me. Though once it was thought dangerous to have too many eggs, research now showed that eggs were low in saturated fat, had lots of healthy nutrients and three types of vitamins. I did, however, balance my omelet with a nutritious salad – just to be on the safe side.

When it got to nine o'clock I was beginning to worry. Surely my mother would not ignore my message.

The phone rang but it was Esther.

'No news, I'm afraid,' I told her. 'I can't believe she hasn't rung me. I wouldn't mind so much but it's now been nearly three weeks since I have spoken to her. That doesn't ever happen usually, even when I'm on holiday.'

'The good thing is that we know where she is. Maybe the message didn't get through or perhaps she went out with some members of her course. Why not just leave it until tomorrow morning and try again then?'

'OK. As you say, we do know where she is and that...hang on, a call is coming through on the other line. I'll speak to you later.'

I hung up on Esther and took the other call. But it was not my mum's number. There was a very quiet muffled voice.

'Mum, is that you?'

I heard a very indistinct 'yes dear'.

'The line isn't very good. Perhaps you can move around a bit?'

'I'm not on my mobile. They take them away at the beginning of the course.'

I now realised that she was indistinct because she was talking in a whisper.

'Why...'

'I'm sorry, I have to go.'

And with that, the phone went dead.

*

'What on earth's happening?' I said to Esther a few moments later. 'And on what kind of course do they take the phones away in the evening as well as during the day?'

'I guess that's what would happen if you went on one of those retreats,' said Esther.

'The receptionist didn't say that she would not be able to use the phone at all.'

'Did Elizabeth sound scared?'

'She didn't sound anything much. She was just whispering. And she didn't say anything more than I just told you.'

'But if she's in real trouble, she would have used the opportunity to ask you to help or contact the police.'

'I suppose that's true.'

'Unless there was someone standing over her while she spoke.'

'What, like in one of those hostage situations?'

'Yes, no... oh, I don't know.'

'You don't think there really was someone standing over her?'

'Isn't it more likely that she was sneaking a phone call on a phone in the B and B and heard someone coming.'

'That's more likely, I think.'

'Let's go to bed and talk in the morning. At least we know she is safe – or kind of safe.'

'I don't mind driving down there now.'

'No, I don't think that's necessary and that is crucially not what your mother asked you to do.'

'Unless she was being coerced on the phone.'

'I still don't think it would be right. I think the thing is, she's not in any immediate danger. In fact, knowing your mother, it may be the other way around.'

That made me laugh.

'Yes, you're right. They have no idea who they are dealing with.'

'OK, night, night. But I'm here if you need me.'

'OK. Night.'

23

When I arrived at the bookshop at 8.30 the next morning, Esther was already there and was sitting and staring intently at one of the computer terminals. She looked up as soon as I came in.

'I have found a few worrying things on social media about this place. Though there are also a few posts lauding it.'

'It's difficult to sort out the fact from the fiction on social media.'

'I know your mum is very capable and I don't want to worry you, but I think you're right to be a little concerned.'

'I think I should go down there.'

'Or perhaps you could just phone and express your concern.'

'Yes, though I have a feeling I know what the answer is likely to be.'

She nodded and we stood together in a dazed silence, trying to make sense of it all, how much we should be worried and unsure about the next move.

Esther finally broke the deadlock.

'This might sound a little crazy but what if I went and booked into the Bed and Breakfast for the night. You don't have to be on the course to book there - I've checked. In fact, it has some good reviews as a B and B. I could suss out what's going on and see if I could speak to you mother.'

'It's not the worst idea in the world.'

'What about contacting the police?'

'What would they say? As far as they are concerned my mother is just attending a life-coaching course but being a bit lax about contacting her son. It hardly constitutes a crime!'

'No.'

'You're right. Perhaps staying in the Bed and Breakfast is a good option. At least we'll be on the spot. The only thing is that I don't think it should be you staying there, it should be me.'

'I suppose we could both go.'

'We couldn't get cover.'

'We could close the shop for one day.'

'No, that would be an overreaction, I think. Let me go down there and find out. After all, even though it all feels a bit weird, it probably is nothing to worry about, really. We just need reassurance.'

This was my second return to the West Country within a few weeks. This time I drove in my old Volvo Estate. I needed a robust big car because of all the collections I had to make of second-hand books. It was a very comfortable drive on the motorway, however, it was not so advantageous on the narrow roads that greeted me as I approached my destination near Glastonbury.

Formidable as my mother was, she had reached her seventieth year (the new 50 she told me), and I was worried that her choice of subject for her project gave her an opportunity for an amount of involvement in situations that may be challenging to her physical and mental health.

I approached the reception desk half-expecting my mother to appear around the corner. Part of me wanted that to happen, but I was also half-terrified at the prospect and my mum's reaction to me being there.

'I understand you also provide life-coaching courses,' I said to the receptionist. 'Is that something you can sample on an overnight stay?'

'No, I'm sorry. They are quite intense courses that require a good deal of commitment. And, I have to say, they're very popular and often book up months in advance. However, I can give you a leaflet on them if it is something you want to consider for the future.'

She sounded like the woman I had spoken to when I rang asking to speak to my mother on the phone.

When I had booked the Bed and Breakfast I had used a different name, Elliot Williams, Esther's surname, so that there would not be an obvious connection between myself and my mother as far as The Beacon was concerned. I had worked out this strategy beforehand with Esther and in a last-minute moment of inspiration Esther had given me her credit card, just in case, 'but make sure you pay me back if you use it', she warned me. I began to panic as I realised that they would probably require ID in this security conscious age, unlike in the past when I would book in for one night with no questions being asked.

The receptionist was chatty and asked me the age-old question of whether I was visiting for business or pleasure. I replied with a lie that I was on my way to Cornwall and that The Beacon made a good stopover point.

'Have you got any ID?'

'I've got my card,' I said.

I showed her Esther's card.

'This is Ms?'

For a moment I toyed with the idea of offering myself as transgender. But I had booked as Mr Williams on the phone so it would have been odd to bring it up now.

'Oh, I'm always doing that. I must have picked up my wife's card by mistake.'

She looked at me a little oddly.

'We are both E Williams, you see.'

'Do you have any other means of identification? Another card or driving licence or passport?'

'I'm sorry I was in a bit of a rush and forgot my driving licence.'

'So, do you have any means of payment?'

'Yes, this should work. Sorry, it's the only card I have. It is the same account. In fact, we share the same pin – we probably shouldn't.'

If she had searched me, she would have found a driving licence and two further credit cards in my pocket.

She looked at me, no doubt unsure whether to go ahead.

'Could I pay now? Then we'll know it's all settled. I can ring my wife, if you like, so that she can authorize it over the phone. She uses Ms rather than Mrs – she's very independent,' I added, though I am not sure if adding that information helped or just made her more suspicious.

Another couple was queuing behind me and someone else was approaching the desk from the entrance. She loaded the amount into the PDQ machine. It was just under the amount for contactless authorization.

'Let's give it a go,' she said.

I spent an uncomfortable moment praying for the card to go through as I did not have the pin.

'Thank you, *Mister* Williams. There's your receipt. Your room is on the first floor, up those stairs.'

She pointed to the right and went on to her next customers. I hurried along.

In the room there was further information about my stay. I was allowed access to the garden and the breakfast room which doubled as an informal lounge in the evenings. There was no restaurant on the premises, but they referred to a nearby pub down the road.

The main part of the building housed the reception. My bedroom and some of the other bedrooms were in a part of the building that purportedly dated back to the sixteenth century. There was also a newer Victorian villa style construction running at right angles to the rest of the house, which I supposed was where the life coaching activities took place. This part of the building had its own entrance gate rather like the type that you find at the bottom of stairwells to prevent toddlers from climbing the stairs. While I was at reception, I had seen a couple of people open the gate and proceed through to the other side of the house.

I returned downstairs to explore the garden. The pattern of dividing the property into two was repeated on the outside. There was a small garden area and a bench. I sat and began reading my book on Coleridge, though I did not take in the words properly as I was more intent on familiarising myself with the surroundings. To my right was a large impenetrable looking hedge with a gate.

I paced around as though taking the air and surreptitiously tried the latch on the gate. It did not give. This was the kind of moment when I wished I still smoked as it would have given me the excuse to wander around with more apparent aimless intent.

At that moment Esther rang.

'How are you getting on?'

I explained about the set-up as I had found it, keeping the phone close to my ear and off speaker.

'It all seems a bit unreal. I'm not sure what I should do next. I have to do something. I can't just go to bed, have my breakfast and leave. Otherwise, what's it all for?'

'Nevertheless, it's reassuring you're there. Give yourself a bit of time, even if it means staying an extra day. I can manage on my own at a pinch. Have you eaten yet?'

'There's a pub they recommend nearby. '

'OK, that's a good idea. The fresh air will do you good. We can talk again later, if you like.'

*

The receptionist confirmed that the pub was an easy walk away. Thankfully, the question of ID no longer came up.

It all seems so incredibly normal, I thought as I strode along. It was as though I was worrying about nothing. And yet, I had not taken that further step that I could have taken, to approach the reception desk and to say that the real reason I was there was to check on my mother and to ensure that she was safe and seek their reassurance. Should that not be the way to approach this? Part of me wanted to but I was also worried about my mother's reaction. This was, after all, part of her research for her project and I did not want to jeopardise it in any way.

Once I arrived at the Wagon and Horses, I ordered my regular pub food favourite, steak and kidney pi e with chips, carrots and peas accompanied by a pint of Exmoor Ale. It was quiet in the pub, and it was the host who brought over my food.

'There you are sir. Are you visiting the area?'

'I'm staying at The Beacon down the road. Do you know it?'

'Ah, yes, I hope you have a comfortable stay.'

'I see they do life coaching courses,' I ventured. 'I'm thinking about something for my mother,' I lied. 'Do you know anything about it?' He paused for a moment. 'I want to make sure it's all right for her. Do you know if it has got a good reputation?'

'As far as I know. You do hear the occasional things but it's difficult to know who to believe. We did have one of those journalists here asking questions about it, but I didn't have anything I could rightly tell them.'

'Oh, I see. Well, sometimes these journalists get funny ideas. Anything for a good story.'

I took my time over my meal, spent some time reading my book and ordered a second pint. One thing I knew was that I was not getting any closer to meeting my mother by staying in the pub. I needed to eat, and the walk was beneficial, but I should get back to see what else I could find out or to try and make contact.

The barman was busy wiping down the bar and clearing up glasses. I put my hand up and thanked him and was about to say goodbye when he walked over to me.

'You were asking about the Beacon. You might have a word with that gentleman over there.' He nodded in the direction of the table in the far corner. 'He came in a while back, as I understand, and was not very happy with his experiences there. Might be worth a word.'

'Thank you, I will.'

'His name's Philip Cartwright.'

I walked across, a little uncertain as to how to make my introduction. I could see a man who was a bit older than me but had obviously been used to an outdoor life, blond and tanned and muscular.

'I'm sorry to interrupt,' I said. He had chosen the same meal as me I noticed. 'My mother is booked on a course for The Beacon and the landlord said you had some experience there yourself.'

He looked up, a little taken aback, not being aware of my presence until that moment.

'My advice is that she should stay away,' he said.

'I'm sorry, did you have a bad experience there?'

I sat down on the opposite seat. He looked me straight in the eye.

'I can tell you a few things, if you like, but you may not like to hear what I have to say.'

'Thank you, I just want to make sure she's safe.'

'My wife died a couple of years ago,' he continued. 'I was at a bit of a loss. I was a marine engineer. I couldn't settle afterwards and wanted to try a new direction. That's when I approached the Beacon. I had got into a bit of a state, drinking too much and being unsociable. They said they could help, and I must admit at the beginning they couldn't have been more friendly. They said what a terrible situation it was to lose someone and that they would try and help me move forward. I felt as though they really cared and supported me. He, Martin that is, used to give me a bear hug and say, *it's all right my friend, you're in our family now*. I feel almost ashamed to admit it now, but it really gave me comfort.'

'Well, a friendly shoulder in time of grief is so important.'

'That was the good bit. Then the meetings and phone calls started. Once or twice a week at first and then every day, weekends as well. He said in order to make real progress, you had to be committed and work hard every day to become a better person, like he was, and he also said that then I would begin making money like him in his financial outfit. He made it sound really noble, like a charitable thing. His company made finance available to people like me who otherwise would not have access to finance. They would hold my hand and make me successful like they had hundreds of other people in the past…'

'I feel a but coming.'

'At the time, it really felt like I was doing something, and it was helping me cope.'

He took a mouthful of beer.

'I know. It's easy to judge these things afterwards.'

'He said it was not an easy path to be successful and required commitment as well as money. He was using his time as he did for lots of people, and he had to cover his costs. He asked for 50,000 pounds to get me to the first level. He said that, though it sounded like a lot of money, it was no more than one good salary for a year and that I would be making far more than that in a couple of years. He also flattered me; said he could see something in me and that I was the sort of person that could really benefit from his coaching. I did have a bit of insurance money but had used it up to pay off the funeral and a few debts, and I had paid off the mortgage. He said the easiest way for me to pay him was to get a loan on the house and once I started making money, I would easily pay it off. I did what he said. He seemed pleased and was really nice to me and hinted at projects that we could do.'

He took a long draw on his pint.

'Then he came back and said that the money I'd given him already was only the first stage and that to reach the important second stage when things really take off, he would need another 50,000. Like a fool I gave it to him. When I started questioning him about when I would see any of the benefits, things got intense. He began criticising me and saying that I was not applying myself properly and he started shouting at me and swearing at me in a way I'd never experienced from him before. Then one day, when I really felt under pressure, I said to him that I was not sure if my wife would have approved. She had been a nurse and a very caring person. Then he said that was what was holding me back, that my wife had been holding me back all those years we had been married and that she was still holding me back even though she was dead. He told me that I had to let her go and forget about my memories of her. He said she had been a malign influence on me and that I was better off without her.'

'How can someone say something like that?'

'That was when I flipped. I told him he was a charlatan and that my wife was the best thing that had happened to me and that she was a far better person than he or I could ever be.'

'I guess that did not go down well.'

'He kept ringing me and tried to say he was sorry, but I refused to speak to him. I knew then that I had been taken in and that he was a fraud. I don't know how I could've been so stupid.'

'You can't blame yourself. You were in a vulnerable position.'

'I asked for my money back, but he said it was too late: I had made a commitment and signed a contract.'

'Had you?'

'Yes, he was always getting us to sign things. Not just for money but also for all the sessions we had.

'When it came to the money, it was just another routine signature. He also had recordings of all our phone calls and conversations, and he said he would make them available to his solicitors if I tried to pursue getting my money back.'

'How terrible. Did you get the police involved?'

'I tried but I'm not getting very far. I'm trying this journalist lady, though, and she seems quite hopeful about being able to do something. No promises mind.'

'I'm so sorry to hear about your case. I hope you can get somewhere with it.'

'If your mother is thinking of one of these courses, my advice is just don't let her do it.'

'I'm afraid it's too late.'

I explained the details and apologised for not being more straight with him and that I thought (but was not certain) that she was there to do some research for her project but that I was worried that I could not contact her.

'That's a typical Martin tactic to take away your means of communication. He makes you powerless. He's a very dangerous man. Your mum might think she can go in there and handle it all right, but he's very persuasive. You find yourself thinking and saying things that you never thought you would.'

'I'm not quite sure what I should do?'

'My advice is whatever you do, keep open the lines of communication. Make sure you can get to speak to her.'

He scribbled down his contact details on a beer mat.

'Contact me if you need to. I'll help as much as I can.'

24

I tried ringing my mother on the walk back from the pub to The Beacon, in case she, by any chance, had access to her phone for the evening - but there was still no reply. It was now starting to get dark. When I got back to the reception area there was no one there. I had it in mind to try and find out my mother's room number. That would mean, though, accessing the computer. The days of the hand-written register were now long gone. I had begun thinking, buoyed up by Philip Cartwright's insistence that I should keep up lines of communication, that the best way forward would be for me to make a scene and insist on seeing my mum. But then, a stroke of luck: there were several A4 printouts on the top of the reception desk headed Coaching Session Rota. I looked down the list. There were names and room numbers, but my mother's name was not there. Damn! I heard the sound of footsteps. I shoved one of the sheets of paper in my pocket suddenly having the thought that there may be more names on the reverse.

'Can I just check what time breakfast is in the morning?' I asked.

'From seven,' she said. 'The last serving is 9.30.'

'Thanks.'

I hurried back to my room hoping that she would not notice that one of her pieces of paper was missing. Once back in my room I looked again down the list and turned it over in the hope I would find more names and my mother's name and room number. Unfortunately, there was no further information on the back. I looked back at the names. Maybe she wasn't taking this course, or she was enrolled in a different one? Then one of the names jumped out at me. There was a name I recognised, the surname White. A common enough name but it was my mother's maiden name.

Margaret White. Margaret was my mother's middle name. Of course, Margaret White. It had to be my mother. Room 24.

A few minutes later, after taking off my shoes in my room, I descended the stairs in my stockinged feet. There was no-one at the reception desk again. There was a bell on the desk, so I guessed that it was not permanently manned at this time of night. I had worked out that the course members rooms must be beyond the gate separating the two sides of the building. I tried the gate but could not get it open. I swung my leg over and, a little awkwardly, made it to the other side.

The numbers of the rooms were in single figures. I walked up to the first floor. The rooms ranged from 10 upwards. I guessed there could not possibly be 20 rooms in the hotel and that the number two prefix just indicated the second floor. When I reached the next floor, I found Number 24 was halfway along on the left-hand side. I tried the door and found that it was unlocked. I called, softly. There was no reply. I sneaked inside the room. I called again but there was still no reply.

I wanted some evidence of my mother having been there, to reassure myself that this was her room. I looked into the top bedside cabinet drawer. There was an opened letter spread out right at the top of the drawer addressed to Margaret White. It began by thanking my mother for taking an enormously important and enlightened step by supporting the principles of the Beacon Foundation. However, the friendly tone of the language became more forthright. I read:

If you do not have separate funding, we recommend raising money from the equity in your house in order to fund further participation in courses at The Beacon. By doing so you will not only be ensuring your own future but fully initiating yourself and providing much needed support for the further establishment and progression of our life-changing organisation. By taking part in this selfless act, you will become part of the extended Beacon Family – the only family you will ever need. It is a family built on mutual respect rather than meaningless blood ties. In participating in this way, you will be taking an important step towards truly freeing yourself and become empowered to lead the life you have always wanted to lead. In order to make this process as straightforward as possible I am enclosing some forms. Please fill them out as soon as you can, and we will pass them on to our firm of solicitors who will put the arrangements in place.

I looked under the letter and in the drawer for the forms but could not see them. I was worried. Had she already filled them in and signed them?

I returned to the letter to see what else it had to say. It ended in a warmer, more complimentary tone.

We would like to express our sincere thanks to you. It is through the enlightened and generous actions of people like yourselves that we are able to put into action our ground-breaking ideas of freedom and personal growth and development. In recognition of this, once the process has been completed, you will be given the status of favoured associate and become an elite member of our organisation, not only benefitting from but also responsible for making decisions on the behalf of others.

On top of the small study table was a clothbound book entitled *Project Diary*. Beneath the heading was written: *Please keep your thoughts about the course here each day and use it as your basis for forming a plan of action. Not to be taken from this room.*

I opened the page. The thought of looking in my mother's personal diary was unnerving. It was not just that I was prying but that I was worried about what I would find out about her deepest thoughts – especially if they concerned me. But what I saw over the next few pages made me start.

The entries were random but sometimes quite long.

Martin is a truly inspirational speaker. He is an unselfish individual whose concerns are not just for us as individuals but for society as a whole. He is an extraordinarily gifted communicator. We all need to get behind him and his personal philosophy and, with commitment, it will make us all rich.

I had a personal interview with Martin today, which I was very excited about. My age, he said, should be no barrier to my success and he said that he admired my spirit and drive to succeed. He said I should not be afraid to take risks. He said he could see me becoming part of his team, as mentor, and that I would bring the wisdom of my life experience with me. To give me this privileged position would require a financial input from myself but, having made that commitment, the rewards would be great. He established with me that I owned a house and asked me the estimated value and said there should be no problem raising the money through an equity release scheme. If I was not good with paperwork, he and his team would help me fill out the forms and all I would be required to do would be to sign my name. I thanked him and said I would give it some thought once I had finished my introductory course. He said that was fine but not to leave it too long as prices tend to go up for the prime places that are available and that there was a great amount of competition to join his mentoring team and that these opportunities did not come along very often.

He asked me about my family, and I told him that I had two sons. He asked me what they thought of me coming here and I said I had not told them as I was worried that they might disapprove. He said that they had no right to disapprove but that, if they did, I should consider breaking ties with them. I said I would find that difficult. He said that he was sure I had been a good mother but that children become influenced by their peers or girlfriends or partners which often makes the relationship with their parents difficult. He said that sometimes it was difficult to let go but that I should think about myself and my own interests and that once I was successful, they would come back to me with open arms. He said it was very important that they are not allowed to hold me back and that they had no right to be involved with any financial decisions. My house was there to use as I needed and not for their own personal gain. They were still young and they would have many opportunities to succeed in their own right. I thanked him and said I would give the whole thing some careful consideration. I asked him what the process was if I wanted to go ahead with the equity release. He gave me his own private email and said that he would be delighted to deal with it himself.

I photographed the pages. My head was reeling. I had no idea my mother could be taken in like this.

I went back to my room and contacted Esther. It was not yet 9 pm.

'I can't believe it,' I said. 'I really think my mother has been seduced by this Somerset cult.'

I texted and attached the photographs I had taken. I followed it up with a phone call.

'Yes, I'm just looking at it,' she said.

There was a long pause.

'Well?' I inquired after what I thought was an age.

'Hang on. I need a bit more time to take this all in. I'll ring you back in five minutes.'

I spent my time looking up The Beacon on the internet and searching for negative comments. I did find one or two just as Esther had, but nothing decisive. I was aware, of course, that the internet was not necessarily the best place to make a faithful judgement of an individual or organization. And I did find some glowing reviews of The Beacon that were, no doubt, put up by friends of The Beacon themselves. And, of course, most damming of all was the testament of the man in the pub.

It was a full five minutes before Esther finally rang back.

'Just before we get into this, where was this diary?'

'It was on the study desk in the room.'

'And do you think it was provided by The Beacon?'

'Yes, it had a printed label on the front encouraging you to put down your thoughts – and telling you not to remove the diary from the room.'

'And this writing in the diary. It's definitely Elizabeth's handwriting?'

'Yes, no doubt about that.'

'Yes, it looks like it to me. Elizabeth does write to me now and again.'

This of itself was a worry to me. I was likely to be the subject of at least some of the words in those letters.

'What occurs to me,' she went on, 'is that this may be Elizabeth's writing, but it's not quite her usual style.'

'I don't know about that.'

'All this "he said, I said". '

'Are you saying my mum is not cultured?'

'No, I'm not saying that. What I am saying is that this is not typical of her writing. Her writing is less prosaic than that.'

'Maybe she has a different writing style when she's writing for essays, or projects.'

'That's possible, but it's not really what I meant. It's like this matter-of-fact style has been deliberately used.'

'You mean she may have been coerced to write it.'

I had visions of Martin standing over her and dictating what she would write.

'No, I don't quite mean that. I think she may have been writing in a particular style for the consumption of the people at The Beacon. You said that the diary was put there by The Beacon and she was encouraged to use it. I don't think they mean for someone to keep it as a personal diary. She may be expected at some point to read from the observations in the diary, maybe even in a public forum to show what a good student she is.'

The penny suddenly dropped.

'Or even, someone from The Beacon may come to the room and look at what they have said and maybe take photos just like I did.'

'I hadn't thought of that. But you're right, they could come and spy on the diary when she was out of the room. It's their way of making sure she is on message.'

'So,using it to see how committed their students are to the cause. That's quite clever.'

'And in her way, this is my reading of it anyway, your mother is being clever by telling them what they want to hear in the hope that they will give away some of the sinister ways in which they operate – which in a way, if you think about it, they already have.'

'Why didn't I think of that?'

'Because you're so worried about her. You're not thinking straight all the time.'

'You're right. I'm not.'

'Of course, I might not be right, and the truth may be somewhere in-between. She might have some admiration for him.'

'I need to speak to her. I'll give it a go now.'

This time I had to wait a while as a group of people were mingling around the area where the gate was, which I needed to climb over in order to gain access to my mother's room.

I caught up on the day's news on my phone while I waited for them to disappear.

This time as I approached room 24, I heard noise, a droning noise. Rather than entering the room I walked to the end of a corridor and there I found an open area and a small balcony, and below, a room full of people. I stepped back, not wanting to be observed. There were about 20 people seated looking towards a man on a raised platform. I scanned the audience. There was my mother in the back row.

From my vantage point, I could see and hear everything clearly. A man, dressed in a sharp suit, was speaking with great enthusiasm and confidence to the small group assembled before him. His voice carried an air of authority, punctuated by persuasive gestures that seemed to mesmerise his audience. He was in full flow. I went closer, though hanging back in the corner so I could escape being seen. I could hear him clearly now. He was talking about success.

'You might be successful; you can be successful. But even if it happens, it might take years – and it might never happen – and you may end up getting a job in Tesco's. OK, someone has to collect those trolleys, operate those checkouts and stack those shelves. But let's leave that to the students and granddads (no offence intended).' There was laughter, the reaction I am sure he intended.

He continued.

'You are the ones that want more than that, whether young or older, you are young at heart and have decided that this is not for you. You may, almost certainly, have had some failures in your life but time is short. The good news is that you don't have to keep making mistakes. You are here because you have made a positive decision. You want success now. You just need a little bit of help with finding your way.' He pointed at his chest. 'My help. But before you invest in this programme which has, by the way, proven to be a wonderful success – you have all seen the video – I must give you one word of warning. You are all capable of achieving great things. We did a pre-assessment when you applied so I have no doubt about that - but it does require hard work and commitment. Not just the commitment of money but of your time and dedication. If you decide to join the program, there will be times when I will ask you to do something which you feel is a little odd or strange - something that does not have an obvious immediate benefit to you. But believe me when I say that these are proven strategies with proven benefits. If you put your trust in me and engage in the full programme following this introductory course the rewards will follow.'

He took a long sip of water before he continued.

'Why me? It is a legitimate question to ask. It is because I have made all those mistakes including some of them that you have not yet made, and I will show you how to avoid them. £50,000 may seem like a lot of money, but ask yourself, is it really? It's one person's good salary for a year. Think about it. One person's good salary for a year in order to make enough money each year for a lifetime. Or what it costs to attend Harvard or Yale. Now, I don't know about you, but I call that a good investment. It's an incredibly good investment. And you will see a return worth that and many times more.'

There was a pause. I could sense him looking around the audience to see if they were with him.

'Now. Before I move on do I have any questions?'

All was silent. He smiled and nodded his head.

'I have one, if I may?'

I saw an arm lifted into the air near the back of the group. It was, of all people, my mother.

'What if, for example, someone was to give £50,000 and then – this is hypothetical of course – what if say there was a problem. You know, someone dies in the family or maybe just changes their mind and wants to become, I don't know, say, an accountant.'

'Of course, good question. And by the way, there are no bad questions. If someone has a particular problem, if someone, for example, dies that is close to you, we would be sympathetic. Because once you join us you are part of the Beacon Family. Yes, we want you to work hard and be committed. Yes, we want you to be successful, yes, we want you to be rich, but we want you to be rich so that you can benefit others. Your wealth will also help enable other people to better their lives. And if you have a tragedy in your life, we want to be there to help you to overcome your grief and recover and go on to the next level.'

At that moment I thought of the man in the pub.

He continued.

'If you decide you want to be an accountant though, I'm sorry I can't help you.'

There was laughter at this point.

'But this does bring up an important point. Thank you again for your question. Once you have made a choice and made your commitment you need to give yourself completely to the task. And I warn you. If you are not prepared to show that commitment now, there is the door,' He gestured with his hand. 'Now is the time to leave.' There was a long pause. 'Anyone want to go and be an accountant? Now is the time to go. Anyone?'

I could hear and sense the shifting of bodies in the chairs, but nobody left. He looked around the room. It seemed as though he was trying to make face contact with everyone there, which must have included my mother, and I had the impression that he looked long and hard in her direction. I saw several in the audience shake their heads and heard a couple of people saying no. It was a few moments before he spoke again, a long dramatic pause.

'Or do you want to come with me on this incredible journey, a journey that hundreds of people have taken before, where they have enriched their lives and made themselves – and others - more financially enriched and,' here he paused for effect, 'more spiritually enriched?'

There was no clapping but much murmuring of assent and the nodding of heads. He smiled. It felt as though he had them at the moment, as though he had absolute control.

'Good, well let's get to it. Tomorrow is the final day of this introductory course where I will explain more about how we start that journey. We have a lot to get through. I will see you all at 9 am sharp and, afterwards, I will see you all individually to discuss the next step or if you have questions or concerns. You need not bring anything with you except alert minds. I have a really good feeling about this group. I am feeling good energy coming from you. I think we can achieve a lot together. Thank you and good night.

Now there was clapping followed by a buzz of excited voices.

I had a dilemma. Should I go to my mother's room and wait for her to come back? It was what I had in mind, but another thought occurred to me. I did not have to check out until eleven the following day. I had not had the presence of mind earlier to make a recording of Martin's speech. If I came back at nine in the morning, I would have that opportunity. I was not certain if my mother was coming straight back to the room but, even if she did, I was not sure how I would be received and of her state of mind and whether I would meet some resistance from her about making a recording. My feeling now was that it was better that I should collect evidence in case I needed to contact the police rather than put all my effort into meeting with my mother immediately.

I resolved to go back to my room to get some sleep and come back and make the recording in the morning. Then I would make an approach to my mother.

25

The next morning, I had breakfast by 8 am, I packed my things ready for checking out and went back to the balcony area. This time I had my phone voice recorder enabled and ready to be switched on, making sure my phone was also fully charged. I was there for the beginning of the session. I could not spot my mum in the audience this time, but I was unable to see everybody without the risk of exposing myself to Martin.

'I'm going to start this session with a poem,' began Martin, 'and I am sorry if I upset any of your sensibilities because it contains a swear word, but it follows on from some of the conversations we have been having recently. I will modify the swear word. The beginning goes:

They eff you up, your mum and dad.
They may not mean to, but they do.
They fill you with the faults they had
And add some extra, just for you.

'That is a poem, as I am sure many of you may be aware, by Philip Larkin called "This Be the Verse". He was right, wasn't he? I have heard several of you report how members of your family, mothers, brothers, sisters, fathers, even your own children – have tried to dissuade you from taking part in this incredible journey with me that we are all on. Not all, by any means, but there are a number of you in that position. And those of you that have family that has encouraged you, and I know there are some of those too, that have given you their support, they should be applauded.

'Let me tell you those members of your family that don't support you are engaging in toxic behaviour. That's right, toxic behaviour. For whatever reason - jealousy, fear of your success or simply that they want to be in control of your life.

And you don't need those people. It may be hard to hear this, but they are holding you back, stopping you from becoming the people you want to be, the people I know you can be, the people they could not be. You just need the freedom to break those shackles. The truth is you don't need them. We are your family now.'

He was walking up and down now, pacing in front of the audience.

'You know there is a spiritual side to our work. I don't believe in one religion. It does not bother me whether you are Christian, Jew or Muslim. There is only one supreme force as far as I am concerned, and we talk to him directly. One side of this spiritual aspect is that by helping ourselves, we are helping others. You may think that by teaching people to succeed we are selfish. Not a bit of it. Not everyone has your ability – to succeed and be successful – and I mean financially as well as spiritually. By being successful you can teach others of a like mind. Being financially successful we help raise up the whole economy so – even those, who for whatever reason, because they aren't as capable as you or don't have your vision – we can help them by helping make the economy more successful for everyone. So, what you are doing now is not just benefitting yourself – and that is important, not just financially and spiritually – but you are benefitting society as a whole. That's quite some thought, isn't it?'

There were a few nods and mumbles.

'You see, this is where we are different. We are socially responsible. By improving ourselves we are improving the whole and acting in concert with that higher and unifying purpose.'

He opened his arms.

'Well, this marks the end of this session. A short workshop session will follow and then each of you will be visited in your rooms for an individual assessment.'

I saved the recording. With all that I had found out I decided to go back to my mum's room to wait for her. A cleaner was just leaving as I approached the door. I turned back on myself, retreated down the stairs and wandered around in the foyer area at the bottom. I gave it a few minutes, looking at my phone as cover in case anybody wondered why I was hanging about on the stairs. When I returned, I saw that the cleaner had moved on to the next room. I took a deep breath and opened the door, hoping that if my mother had already returned to her room, I would not give her a heart attack. There was nobody in the bedroom. The bathroom door was open.

'Mum,' I said in a loud whisper.

A towel was neatly folded and placed at the end of the bed, which was made. There were no clothes scattered around. All was neat and tidy. There was something else, something different I could not quite put my finger on.

Ah, yes, I knew what it was now. The diary was missing. Perhaps she had gone somewhere to write it up. I sat down on the bed for a moment. I considered wandering into the garden. I might bump into her there.

Just as I got up and was about to leave, I heard the sound of rapid footsteps which I guessed were not those of my mother. I judged I was too far away from the bathroom to make it before someone entered the room. I swung my legs over to the far side of the bed and dropped down between the bed and the wall.

There was a knock at the door.

'Mrs White?'

I edged my way under the bed so that I would be completely out of sight as I heard someone entering the room.

'Mrs White,' I heard again. I could hear what I thought were two people moving about the room. Then I heard another voice.   It was the unmistakable voice of Martin.

'Is she not here?'

'No. I'll ring reception.'

There was a pause and then a moment later:

'Can you tell me if you've seen Mrs White this morning? We didn't see her at our 9 am meeting.'

So that was why I could not see her that morning when I made the recording. She was not there at all.

'The receptionist says she's not checked out,' the other man said.

'Ask her if her car is there.' said Martin.

There was a long pause.

I heard pacing up and down. Then it stopped. I could hear more talking on the phone but this time I could not hear what was being said.

Then I heard their voices again. It felt as though Martin was right next to me.

'No car,' I heard the other man say.

'So, her car's gone but the receptionist didn't know she had left. How can that be?' said Martin.

'She didn't check out of reception. That's odd.'

'Yes, strange. I had high hopes she would do the next level course.'

'Maybe she just got nervous about the debriefing. Or there might have been some family crisis.'

'I think we'd better handle this carefully. There was a lot of potential there. She owned her own home so was in a position to finance a further course and maybe make a substantial contribution. I'll see if I can get in touch with her later and invite her back. A bit of a charm offensive may be in order here.'

'She won't have been able to get her phone anyway. It's locked in the safe.'

'And she will want that.'

'Maybe it was a family crisis.'

'But how would she have known if she didn't have access to her phone?'

'Who was covering the night reception?'

'Check, can you? Someone might have rung reception – oh, and check to see if there are any written messages left on reception that might have been missed.'

'I'll do it right away.'

I was getting hot in my position under the bed - and feeling a little claustrophobic. I waited but it seemed that Martin was in no hurry to leave the room. I heard him walking up and down again. Then he stopped. There was silence for several minutes. Perhaps he had left the room? But I had not heard the door open or close or any retreating footsteps. I was thinking about moving out from my position under the bed but just at the moment I heard him sit down quite heavily, with an accompanying sigh. The bottom of the bed bowed under his weight.

I had a vision of him saying, I *know that you are there lying right beneath me.*

What would I say in return?

Oh, just checking the underside of the bed to make sure it's in good order.

Why did I come up with these bizarre thoughts?

There were footsteps again. The other man had returned.

'I've checked reception. No messages. I also got in touch with Ruby.' He gave a cynical laugh. 'She wasn't too happy as she'd not been off her shift very long, but she said it had been a very quiet night and that she didn't remember hearing a car pulling out. I also checked the safe for good measure – her phone was still there...'

'She's taken the diary, though.' He did not sound pleased. 'It's clearly marked as our property. She shouldn't have done that. I'm not happy about that. It's not hers to take.'

'Perhaps she intended to write up some entries later.'

'OK, let's leave it for now and go on to the next one. We'll come back to this later.'

I heard them leave but was reluctant to come out straight away and made myself wait another minute or two, in case one of them returned to the room having left something behind.

Finally, I convinced myself it was safe and extricated myself from my position and dusted myself down. I crept out of the room and made my way back to the gateway. It was slightly out of sight of reception, and the receptionist was pre-occupied serving a customer. I swung my leg over the gate and walked to the right towards my room. I took a few moments to ensure that I had not left anything behind and then went to check out.

The receptionist appeared to be under stress, no doubt because of my mother's sudden disappearance. She forwent all the usual niceties about whether I'd had a good stay and took the key from me after having confirmed that there was nothing extra to pay.

I went over to my car and was about to turn on the ignition key when my phone rang.

It was mother.

26

'I'm sorry if I've been a bit elusive,' she began.

She then proceeded to tell me how she had registered for the course, 'undercover', using her maiden name for which she had retained a separate bank account after her marriage, all those years ago.

'But why did you leave early?'

'I didn't trust myself to stand the pressure of his final briefing. I wasn't sure I was up to it and that I wouldn't give myself away. Besides, I have so much material for my project already.'

I then told her about how I had stayed at the Bed and Breakfast and recorded some of the lecture.

'I'd no idea you were there,' she said. 'That recording could be useful for my project, though. Can you send it to me?'

'But what about your phone you left behind and all your contacts?'

'No contacts of importance. It was a just cheap old pay as you go thing I bought at the supermarket. They can do what they like with it as far as I'm concerned.'

'Who would have thought my own mother was using a burner phone?'

'Anyway, I'm a bit tired now,' she continued. 'And my head is fizzing with all the information. I'll let you know more about it later on.'

'It's just good to know you're safe.'

When I spoke to Esther later, she was delighted that my mother had arrived home safely, while at the same time she was worried about the extent of her involvement.

'I wonder how she's going to use this information,' she said. 'It's one thing writing about historical cults. But ones that are still current. Might she not be in danger?'

'My mother was never one to shy away from an argument.'

'I just hope that she has not taken on too much this time.'

'So do I.'

'There's no rush to get back by the way. Aggie is here for the rest of the day, and it's as quiet as anything.'

'In that case, you know what I may do. I'm not far from Glastonbury. I think I might visit the Tor before I come home. It's something I've always wanted to do but never quite got round to.'

27

I left the car park in Glastonbury and headed towards the middle of the town and immediately felt a different vibe. People were dressed in striking colours and the smell of incense was everywhere. Perhaps it helped that the sun was shining but everyone seemed to be in a positive and welcoming mood. I felt I could slow down a bit and take my time.

I wandered into well-stocked bookshops that carried a dazzling array of esoteric books. There were also shops specialising in various paraphernalia relating to goddesses, witches, faeries and ancient artefacts. I was taken aback by the striking frontage of The Tribunal, an extraordinary characterful building dating back to the fifteenth century. It was like something you may expect to see in a *Harry Potter* film.

I learned that it was called The Tribunal because it was thought that at one time court proceedings took place there. It was also, in its time a merchant's house, a shop, a school and a convent. It was now a museum. I decided to give it a quick visit. Inside was a fascinating display of artefacts from a Glastonbury Iron Age village on the Somerset levels about three miles away.

After leaving the museum, I started my walk out of town towards the Tor, on my way visiting The Chalice Well. The well, I read, has been in constant use for over 2,000 years with water issuing from the spring at 25,000 gallons a day and, apparently, it had never failed. In Christian Mythology the well marks the site where Joseph of Arimathea, who assumed responsibility for the burial of Jesus, placed the chalice that caught the drops of Christ's blood at the Crucifixion. Whether there was any truth in the myths surrounding The Chalice Well, I found the atmosphere of the garden with its pools of water a calming experience.

I began ascending the first of the seven terraces that needed to be negotiated to reach the top of the Tor. Once I had reached the second terrace, I looked back down on the way I had come. Beneath me on a piece of open ground was a group exercising and chanting. I took my time as I walked up the remainder of the terraces. I was eventually welcomed at the top of the hill by two women playing the bodhran. I watched as they built up to a crescendo before emitting a primal scream.

The tower at the top, I had read beforehand, is the remains of St Jonathan's Church built in the 14th century. It had survived until the dissolution of the monasteries in 1539. All except the tower was demolished. It was also, chillingly, the place of execution of the last abbot of Glastonbury, Richard Whiting, hung, drawn and quartered along with two of his monks, John Thorne and Roger James.

What many people know the Tor for now, though, is its spiritual incarnation as The Isle of Avalon, as it was called by the Britons and, for some, it is The Avalon of Arthurian legend. According to Gerald of Wales, the coffins of King Arthur and Queen Guinevere were discovered here in 1191. It is also claimed to be the location of the Holy Grail and, more recently, of the goddess movement.

As if to reflect this, inside the tower at that moment was a woman dressed in a robe chanting and praying. I carefully stepped by her and sat on an area of stonework on one side for some minutes, not wanting to be denied my own moment of reflection. After some moments of contemplation, I looked up into the tower and narrowly avoided being covered in droppings from the birds that had gathered there. I took this as my cue to leave and spent some time circling around the top of the hill and taking in the magnificent view. Whatever the truth of the myths and legends surrounding the Tor, I could feel the magic of its setting within the landscape.

A call came through on my phone flashing Laura's name.

'Have you got a moment?' she said.

'Yes.'

I explained that I was on top of Glastonbury Tor.'

'Like the festival?'

Everyone in the world had heard of Glastonbury Festival.

'Yes.'

'Well, I thought I would give you an update on how things are progressing at this end.'

'Oh, yes.'

'I dolt know how significant it is but it seems that Cantalbrini has two sons, and one of them, Georgio, who I mentioned to you before, lives in the UK.'

'Is there any evidence that he deals in books?'

'Let's say there is circumstantial evidence that hasn't yet been verified.'

'Where can we go from here? Do you have a photo?'

'Yes, but not a recent one. I am sending you one over, but it's of him as a child. You know, it's one of those Facebook entries of his younger self.'

It came through to my WhatsApp at that moment.

'Well, ah yes. It could be but then, I suppose he must only be five or so in this photo.'

'Given some time I think the police I should be able to get a driving licence or passport photo. I have just been so busy the last few days and haven't had a chance to liaise with Alessandro.'

'I'm sorry to bother you when you're busy.'

'No, really, it's OK. You said you thought they knew you were taking *Lyrical Ballads* down to the West Country from your Facebook page?'

'Yes, we use it quite a lot for promoting books and talks and so on. I didn't agree with it, but Esther thought it would be fun to advertise my walk. Even though I sent the books ahead by courier, from the Facebook page you could get the impression I was taking them down in person.'

'And it would not at all be unlikely that having met you in Italy Cantalbrini would then look you up on social media.'

'Yes.'

'Do you know if he does follow you?'

'I did a quick search but couldn't find anything. But we do have a couple of thousand followers and it's quite likely that he isn't using his own name.'

'Yes, of course.'

'And if Georgio is the man that stole my rucksack...'

'And pushed you off the cliff.'

'Which now seems like it's a possibility. What happens next?'

'I think the police will get you to make a definite identification from a photo and then they'll need to track Cantalbrini's son down and take him in for questioning. I suspect it's unlikely that the police will get Cantalbrini to admit that he instructed his son to assault you, but the circumstantial evidence may be too overwhelming.'

'You know, I wish it wasn't like this. You probably think this is strange, but part of me still likes Cantalbrini. And I think what a waste of all that knowledge. If I had been braver and refused to accept his gift of *Lyrical Ballads*, none of this would have happened.'

'But then, further down the line, someone else would have been involved in a similar situation.'

'I suppose so.'

'You have to ask yourself, would you have ever acted in that way?'

'No, never, well I hope not.'

'That's what you have to tell yourself. It's unacceptable behaviour. I have sympathy with those who simply want to send books abroad without all the bureaucracy and expense of the export licence but knowingly accepting stolen goods and being implicated in someone's murder because they are threatening to expose you. That is much more than just bending the rules.'

'I might have sold a few books for more than they are worth once or twice.'

'That's what we call clever marketing in Italy! Anyway, let's see where it takes us.'

'At least we might have an answer to why I was attacked and who by. That's a kind of comfort in itself.'

'I have another call trying to get through. I'd better go, but what's that noise in the background.'

I explained about the playing of the bodhran.

'You'll hear a primal scream in a moment.'

I pointed the phone in the direction of the two players in anticipation.

'Wow,' she said that's some scream! Better go. Ciao.'

'Ciao.'

I made my way back down to the bottom of the Tor, a much easier and quicker journey than coming up, and made my way back towards the town centre. I had another half an hour in the car park. I ordered a coffee at one of the cafés and grabbed a local newspaper from a nearby shop while I was waiting. I wanted to absorb something more of the local flavour before I left Glastonbury.

Just as my coffee arrived, I was taken aback by a headline in the newspaper. It read: "Tragic Death of Young Man". It described the death of Michael Cassio, Desdemona's son. Sadly, he had not recovered from his coma.

I texted Jonathan to pass on my commiserations.

28

Next morning I was back working with Esther at the bookshop. I told her about the sad death of Michael Cassio.

'So sad. Was it suicide do you think?'

'There were drugs involved but whether it was an overdose or an accident I don't know. He was certainly very troubled, according to Jonathan and Dora.'

'Poor boy.'

We divided up the work for the morning between us. Esther would handle customers and orders while I would catalogue books. We worked side by side.

I returned to the subject of my mother.

'I wonder if she slept well last night. She told me she had much more to tell me. Perhaps I should ring her later,' I said.

'Better than that. She can tell you yourself. She's coming on Friday.'

'What? She didn't tell me.'

'She rang me last night. I was going to tell you when you came in this morning, but you had that awful news about that poor boy. She needs someone to share the information with. I have my spare room sorted now so she can stay with me if it's easier.'

'But why didn't she ring me?'

'She was worried she had upset you – and all that trouble you went to, going to see her – even though you didn't.'

'That's not quite true. I did see her ask a question.'

'You know, formidable as your mum is, she's a bit afraid of you.'

'What? Not really. I don't believe that. But really, I think it's best if she stayed with me.'

'I think that's best too, especially as you have a bit more room – but I was happy to offer if it was difficult.'

'But you will come and eat with us?'

'Yes, of course. Don't worry, I won't leave you to face the burden of looking after your mother on your own.'

As I was walking home after work my phone made a noise. It was another photo from Laura.

'Is this anything like him?' the accompanying text said.

I saw the photo of a man, perhaps in his late twenties or early thirties with long blond hair and a moustache and beard.

I rang Laura.

'Nothing like him I'm afraid.'

'I thought that may be the case.'

'He's changed a lot since the photo of him as a youth.'

'You don't think he could have cut his hair and dyed it black since?'

'No, his mouth and lips are much fuller, and he has a wide forehead. The man who pushed me had a much slimmer frame and a narrow forehead. I don't think he can be the same person as the one who attacked me.'

'It's a shame but it doesn't necessarily let Cantalbrini off the hook.'

'Really?'

'Well, he may have another contact in the UK rather than his son – or it may still be his son working in concert with someone else in the UK.'

'So, his son could still be involved in some way?'

'Possibly. I think there's definitely more work we can do on this. I'll talk with Alessandro and no doubt he will talk to the British police.'

'It all seems so unreal now. I wonder if it's worth pursuing. I think I'm getting over the experience at last.'

'Well, as you probably know, lots of crimes are never resolved, but I think we should pursue this a little further.'

'OK, I will take your advice. And thank you for your support and for taking it seriously.'

'Not at all.'

'Do you know about Cameron's history book he's writing?'

Cameron and Laura were friends for a year at university in Manchester.

'Yes, isn't it exciting?'

'Perhaps that's the time you should come and visit.'

'Yes, I would like that.'

I had a backlog of work processing new and second-hand books and catching up with customer enquiries and some large school orders that had come through with the approach of the autumn term. It meant I had to stay and work late at the bookshop. I felt quite exhausted by the time Friday morning came and, I had to admit, was looking forward to an evening of self-indulgence, perhaps a film and a glass of wine, when Esther said, 'You haven't forgotten your mother is coming?'

Of course I had. I had so successfully pushed the idea of her visit to the back of my mind that it had totally disappeared.

'Only temporarily,' I said, which I suppose was the truth.

'I'll bring her over to you as she is popping round to see me first.'

'Oh, OK'

'So, what are you feeding us this evening?' I was aware that I was looking blank. 'You do remember that you invited me around to dinner. In fact, you insisted on it.'

'Of course, of course.'

'So, what's it going to be, one of your nifty lasagne's? Did you prepare it last night? I always feel they taste better when left for a day. Or is it one of your delightful stews?'

'Well, I think I would rather leave it as a surprise.'

In my own mind, up to that point, the only cooking I was going to do that evening was a pizza from the freezer accompanied by a few glasses of wine – the typical bachelor standby.

At the end of the day, I walked home via the supermarket. I could not get my head around cooking anything for Esther and my mum. Lasagne was too much of an effort and, as Esther implied, I always felt a lasagne was not something that could be rushed and benefitted from sitting around. The same applied to stew and, in any case, it felt too hot for stew. So, I took inspiration from my recent visit to Jonathan and Dora. I would bake some potatoes and provide a selection of meats and cheeses and salads. They could have as much or as little they wanted.

As soon as I reached home, I shoved some potatoes in the oven, left the cheese out to breathe and washed the salad. I was aware that the most onerous task was not the food but all the other preparations I would have to make before my mum's visit.

I only cleaned when someone came to visit. Otherwise, the only hoovering I did was to press on a little robot hoovering machine in the lounge once a week (mainly to pick up remnants of pizza or salad) and it was ages since I had changed the sheets in the spare bedroom where my mum was going to sleep. In fact, I was pretty sure I had not changed the sheets since the last time she had stayed. No mow May was also long gone, and though I had decreased the size of my lawn considerably, what was left was in sore need of a trim.

So, after an hour of intense rushing around hoovering with a proper vacuum cleaner, right into the corners and all around the house and especially in the spare bedroom, replacing the sheets on the spare bed and putting the ones I had taken off the bed in the wash, cutting the lawn and finishing preparing the meal, I decided on a quick shower. Of course, Esther and my mum turned up while I was still in there. I shouted from the bathroom window and suggested they let themselves in.

Esther had settled Mum into her room by the time I had finished.

I brought the food through to the table in my small dining room. Esther led the conversation as we dished up our dinner.

'What an adventure you've had,' she said to my mum.

'Yes, I'm sorry I led you all such a merry dance.'

I refrained from saying that this was the understatement of the year.

'We were just worried about you,' I said. 'If only you'd told us beforehand.'

'I was afraid you might...'

'Yes...'

'Try and stop me.'

'When have I ever succeeded in stopping you from doing anything?'

'Well...'

'You can be very disapproving sometimes,' chipped in Esther.

As usual, when I was in Esther and my mum's presence together, I felt ganged up upon.

'But then, this food was a great idea.'

'Yes, Mum agreed. I've never thought of you as a cook.'

'This isn't really cooking; it's just throwing stuff together. Anyway, why don't you tell us some more about this operation at The Beacon?'

'That's good Elliot,' said Esther, 'from now on when we refer to it, I think we should call it *Operation Beacon*.'

'I think you may have gathered quite a lot of it when you recorded that speech but, in essence, I think it's a way of taking people's money while pretending to help them with life coaching.'

'So, all that stuff about him being a brilliant speaker that you wrote in your diary…'

'He is a brilliant speaker; there's no doubt at that… you heard him. But the other things I wrote about him being wise… that was for their consumption. I knew that's what they wanted me to say.'

'They were very annoyed about you taking the diary.'

'I would've photographed it, but I didn't have access to my phone – and, in any case, it doesn't have a camera. I've already sent it back to them, apologising.'

I repeated a phrase I had used earlier.

'I never thought I would have a mother who used a burner phone.'

'I think that was a stroke of genius,' said Esther.

My mum smiled coyly and then was quiet for a moment.

'You know there was another person undercover at The Beacon. She left the day after me.'

'What?'

'Yes, someone called Angela. At least, that was the name I knew her by.'

'Was she MI5?'

'No, don't be daft. She was working for a newspaper.'

I had a crazy thought. Perhaps hardly any of the twelve on the course were genuine course members. Perhaps there was the BBC, The CIA and even the KGB – or whatever they were called now.

'She left the day after me. She's uncovered some really interesting stuff.'

'But how did you know to trust her?'

'She invited us to contact her when the course was finished, said that she would like to keep in touch. I was reluctant at first, but I gave her my old email address that doesn't have my name on it and gets forwarded to my main email. Then a couple of days after the course ended, I got this email saying I see you left the course early. I wondered if you were dissatisfied in any way. I have a few misgivings myself. Would you mind if I spoke to you on the phone? I was really unsure.'

'How exciting,' said Esther.

'I wasn't convinced that it wasn't a ruse and wondered if she might be working for The Beacon. I left it a couple of days before I replied. Then I plucked up the courage to speak to her on the phone. When she spoke to me, I was a little evasive and said my main reason for following the course was to get a better understanding of the module I was doing. She said she was also doing some research, and would I be able to help her with a few questions and could we compare notes. That's when I asked her if I could trust her and she sent me the details of the newspaper she was working for.'

'You may be able to get your project mentioned in her newspaper.'

'I don't know about that but that was when things got really interesting. I met her at her newspaper offices, and we have been able to exchange some information. I may be able to use some of the information she has found on my own account in my project, properly referenced, of course.'

'Wow,' said Esther.

'We are a bit worried about any reprisals there might be if you write about a current cult,' I said.

'It will only be a part of my project. Quite a lot of it will be in a historical context. I am also researching other cults like The Jesus Army and The Children of God. Though, there's no doubt this will be an important aspect of it as it is original research. And my tutor will give me guidance.'

'Well, as you're here perhaps you can come to Simon's grand gathering,' I suggested.

'I have Chloe coming too,' said Esther. 'Did you know Simon is actually providing her with a room to stay in?'

'Actually,' said my mother, 'I wondered if I could ask you another favour? Angela, my journalist friend is coming through the area tomorrow and wants to discuss things.'

'Great, the more the merrier,' said Esther. 'I can put her up.'

29

The meeting at Simon's, originally conceived as a progress report on his steps to become more ecologically friendly, had morphed into a kind of country house weekend.

Those present were Chloe (Esther's friend), Esther, Aggie, Angela (my mum's journalist friend), my mum (Elizabeth), Simon, Miriam and myself.

This was the August bank holiday weekend, and we always closed the bookshop on bank holidays which gave us two full days free.

Aggie picked up me, my mother and Angela and then we proceeded to Esther's. It was a bit of a squeeze in her Citroën Dyane. Mum, in respect to her age, sat in the front while Esther, Angela and I squeezed in the back.

'I'm not sure if it was ever designed for five people,' said Aggie but, somehow, we managed.

We found Chloe and Simon already at work in the garden at the back of the house just beyond a fine looking hen-house (yet to acquire any chickens). There were several wooden crosses in the ground with names of apples on them.

Esther and Chloe gave each other a big hug, and I shook hands with Chloe, reacquainting myself after our trip to see her earlier in the year.

Angela and my mother were introduced to Simon.

'No Max?' I said, referring to Chloe's young son.

'No, he's with his father. At last, I get my freedom.'

'We've just about finished here,' said Simon. 'Time for coffee, I think.'

But we lingered a while to show my mum and Angela the extensive garden and to outline some of Simon's plans.

Esther and Aggie disappeared into the kitchen to help Miriam with making the coffee and soon returned with two large cafetieres and a tray of cups and milk and sugar.

We sat around in chairs in an informal semi-circle.

'So, have you got your apples sorted then?' I asked Simon.

'Very nearly. I think it's best if Chloe explains.'

'It does depend quite a lot on the local climate,' said Chloe but, basically, we'll be starting with The Beauty of Bath. It depends on the season, but it's usually ready in early August or sometimes even late July. Then a bit later,' she looked at Simon, 'I think we are looking at things like Discovery and Worcester Pearmain.'

'I know those, very tasty,' said my mother.

'Then in October we'll have Cox's Orange Pippin and Braeburn. Then going into to late October there's a variety called Fuji – very sweet – and then, to finish, for November we are planting Jazz. I think that's about it isn't it, Simon?'

'Isn't she brilliant,' said Simon. 'You were so right to recommend her, Esther.'

'Of course, we haven't mentioned cooking apples and plums yet.'

'We'll get onto those later,' said Simon.

'Now, I know Miriam doesn't like anyone in the kitchen, but Elliot and I insist on helping, don't we Elliot?' Esther announced.

I had no forewarning of this but had no alternative but to say yes.

Simon had to take a trip into town to fill up with petrol and get a few essentials before dinner and he took Chloe with him so they could continue their conversations about fruit.

'I feel like my vegetable input has been abandoned to Chloe and her fruit trees,' said Aggie.

My mother and Angela were already in deep conversation about The Beacon.

'I think I will join you in the kitchen,' said Aggie to Esther and me.'

We were conscious of not getting in Miriam's way as she prepared the dinner. I did menial things like chopping carrots while Esther was allowed more direct responsibility, like helping prepare the Yorkshire puddings.

'Why don't you have a look at Simon's library?' said Miriam to Aggie as she stood at one end of the kitchen not quite sure what to do. I showed her where it was. I knew she would be able to spend a happy hour there.

Dinner preparations seemed to move quickly after that, and soon I was preparing the table outside with cutlery and glasses and a jug of water.

Simon had returned and it was not long before we were all sitting around the large table outdoors. It was a traditional Sunday roast of roast beef but with a nut roast alternative and a dizzying array of various vegetables, boiled, roasted or fried.

'You must tell us about your adventures,' said Simon to my mother and Angela.

'Where to begin?' said my mother.

'Well, let's begin with your project, Elizabeth.' said Angela.

'As some of you know, my project as part of a Religion and Ethics course is on New Religions, more commonly known as cults. I have been looking at it in a historical context which is why I was interested in the Agapemonites, the Abode of Love at Spaxton near where Elliot was going on his walk. There are some people still alive that remember it before it finally closed. But, as you know, they like original research for a project. When I was researching it, someone tipped me off about this life-coaching place at The Beacon, how there had been some stories about it.'

'But this is life coaching not a religious cult,' said Simon.

'Simon, let her finish,' said Miriam.

'No, that's a good point. But there seemed to be some similarities between this life coaching course and what you find in cults and the coercion they go in for. Though it does not claim to be a religious set-up he does invoke a higher power without naming it as God or any particular religion. Anyway, I thought that it was too good an opportunity to miss to do some original research, so I signed up for the course.'

'Undercover and with a burner phone. Can you believe it?' I exclaimed.

'Your mother is very resourceful,' said Angela.

'That's what I was about to say,' said Esther.

'Anyway, Angela can tell you more about it as she did the same thing at the same time as me – and she's been researching it for months.'

'I would say it does count as a cult,' said Angela. 'A truly beneficial life-coaching course is about empowering the individual. This is all about coercion and control.'

'Is there any evidence that it has done any real harm?'Chloe asked.

'Yes. Though there's a video talking about its successes, those that it claims as successes are really people it has recruited as its disciples to recruit yet more people. Its biggest success I would say is in extracting money to take further courses.'

'Like many universities nowadays,' Aggie said.

'But these are large sums of money. He tried this on you, didn't he, Elizabeth?'

Angela turned to her.

'Yes, he wanted me to get an equity loan of £50,000.'

'There are cases of people taking the course and losing their house because of it. And they will often come back for more. When someone asks for their money back or claims the course is not working, they start blaming the course attendee for not putting enough effort in and things often end badly. They also have this really nasty aspect where they turn people against their own family if they are not supportive. The worst case I came across was where they told someone to stop taking their medicine for depression. He went and committed suicide.'

I thought of Michael Cassio at that moment even though it was in a different context.

'Can't they be closed down?' asked Miriam.

'That's what we're hoping to achieve but it's a long process and we have to be careful to do all our research properly. The trouble is with life coaching courses, anyone can set one up without any professional qualifications.'

'Well, let's hope you're successful,' said Miriam.

'We'll drink to that,' said Simon, giving the first of many toasts that day.

'Of course, Elizabeth's research is invaluable and will no doubt get a mention,' said Angela.

'Well done,' said Esther.

'And Angela has agreed to share some of her research with me.'

'I think I see a distinction coming,' said Aggie.

My mother blushed for the first time, I suspect, in many years.

'So that takes care of that,' said Simon. 'But now you must tell us about your adventures in the Quantocks, Elliot.'

'I don't know if there is anything much to tell,' I said.

'Oh, come on,' said Esther.

'Beyond,' I continued, 'that I had a lovely walk along the Coleridge Way and met some very nice people at the Coleridge Society.'

'Nobody murdered on this trip?' said Aggie.

'Aggie!' said Esther. I think that was the first time I had ever heard Esther admonish Aggie for anything.

'In fact,' said Esther, 'a poor boy lost his life to a drug overdose while Elliot was there. And Elliot was pushed off the edge of the cliff and was lucky not to lose his life.'

Up to now, nobody except Esther knew about this among the present company.

There was a collective gasp and Aggie said she was sorry.

'I don't think he meant to push me off the cliff,' I said. 'He stole my rucksack. He pushed me when he grabbed my rucksack, and I couldn't stop myself falling over.'

'Who pushed you?' asked Simon.

'That's it. We don't actually know,' I said.

'We think it may have been organised by Cantalbrini, you know the bookseller in Rome,' said Esther.

'It's complicated. He gave me *Lyrical Ballads* but I think it was to buy my silence about the connection between Mr Abruzzio and himself.'

I was aware that Chloe and Angela knew nothing about this story, so I explained a bit more, about how Cantalbrini was implicated in the murder of Mr Abruzzio and how he had tried to buy my silence by gifting me the *Lyrical Ballads* books.

'So, they were trying to steal them from you before you ended your walk?' said Angela.

'Yes, except I didn't have them. I'd sent them on ahead by courier – but we think they thought I had them.'

'I know it sounds crazy now,' said Esther, 'but I was putting posts on Facebook about him taking a valuable version of

Lyrical Ballads to its spiritual home. That's how they knew where Elliot was on the journey and the timings.'

'They did steal another book I had in there, probably thinking initially it was the correct book – and a credit card – so it could just be a regular thief – but nothing's proven.'

'So, not a murder but an attempted murder,' said Angela.

'A possible attempted murder,' I said.

'But, in any case, a mystery,' said Aggie.

'A crime was committed,' said Chloe.

'An assault,' said Angela. 'that's a crime in itself.'

'And theft,' added Simon, 'of the book and the credit card.'

'And it remains a mystery,' I said. 'The police have been involved, both here and in Italy, but have not come to any definite conclusion. And perhaps never will.'

'We're calling it a *Somerset Odyssey*: Elliot's journey and his troubles and his acquisition of wisdom about Coleridge,' said Esther.

'And now, no doubt, returning to slay Penelope's lovers,' added Aggie who looked pointedly at Esther.'

'Oh, do tell me who they are,' said Chloe conspiratorially to Esther taking up Aggie's thought process while at the same time embarrassing me with the clear implication that I was Esther's lover.

'Later,' said Esther.

My phone which was on the table, bleeped.

'Another post from one of my Coleridge friends on Facebook. Oh no,' I said. 'They've posted a photo of Michael Cassio.'

His dark Latin-like features stared back at me from the phone.   The mystery had been solved. It was, I now realised, Michael Cassio who had pushed me off the cliff.

Epilogue

I contacted the police in Lynton and had an interview on Zoom where I testified that the photo of the man I now knew as Michael Cassio was the person that I recognised as pushing me off the cliff. They said they would speak to the Italian police in Rome.

I also rang Laura.

'So, it seems that Cantalbrini – or his son or his cohorts – were not responsible.'

'I was so convinced at one stage that it could not be anything else. Perhaps he genuinely wanted to give me *Lyrical Ballads* as a gift.'

'But why?'

'Because he liked me?'

It sounded strange even as I said it. I had only known him a few days, after all.

'He may well have liked you, but I still think your original idea was right about keeping silent about your knowledge of his relationship with Mr Abruzzio. You have to realise how common it has been in Italy to put pressure on witnesses to remain silent.   He may have also seen you as someone who could help him import books into the UK.'

'It begs the question, why he has not been in touch in some way to get *Lyrical Ballads* back?'

'Yes, well I suppose that is why we believed he could have been responsible in the first place. You have given the books away to a worthy cause. Maybe he accepts that – if he even knows - or he just has too many things to preoccupy his mind at the moment. But who knows really?'

'In some ways it may have been preferable that it was him. I feel so sorry for poor Cassio.'

'Yes, it is all very tragic.'

I rang Jonathan and Dora to explain that Michael Cassio was responsible for attacking me. Both of them were, of course, surprised by the news. They suggested I did a video message to them so we could all speak together.

'I feel so sorry for Cassio,' I said again after we had started the call. 'I can't help blaming Desdemona for pushing the drugs on him.'

'Desdemona is inconsolable,' said a tearful Dora. 'She does blame herself. This will make her feel even worse. She thought she was helping to cure his stuttering by giving him drugs. It may not have been the right thing to do. But she did think she was helping.'

'There's no doubt she could be reckless. That's part of her character,' said Jonathan. 'But even so, she's a friend of ours. She has a good heart and there is no doubt that she loved Cassio.'

'Though we are sorry for you, of course,' said Dora.

'I feel quite angry about Desdemona's part in this,' I said to Esther a little later. 'She as good as killed him.'

Esher was quiet.

'I'm not so sure.'

'What?'

'She thought she was helping.'

'By getting him addicted to drugs!'

'By curing his stuttering. She may not have been the perfect mother but from what you tell me she really seems to have cared in her own way. I really don't think you can blame her outright. You can be sure she's suffering more than anyone right now. She may not have done the right thing, but what she needs right now is compassion and understanding.'

Esther's observations had made me question my view of the situation. I kept coming back to the fact that I knew so little of Cassio. But he had attacked me and pushed me off the cliff. I felt I needed to know more about him.

I asked Jonathan and Dora if I could go and visit them at the weekend.

'I know it may sound a strange request, but I feel if I knew more about him, I could better cope with the idea of him attacking me.'

'Of course, my dear friend,' said Jonathan. 'In truth we are having trouble trying to come to terms with it ourselves. Dora and Desdemona are close friends and have been for many years.'

I drove down to them and was with them within a couple of hours, in time for a late lunch.

'Cassio was an only child, and Desdemona was so busy herself,' said Dora as we began our lunch. 'It became very difficult when his father left. I remember he was left with a series of child minders and play groups. She was always getting into trouble for being late. We looked after him sometimes.'

She turned to Jonathan.

'Yes, he was always a quiet boy and used to play alone a lot of the time.'

'He didn't seem to make many friends, which is strange when you think how gregarious Desdemona is,' said Dora.

'Sounds like he was left on his own an awful lot.'

'Yes, but of course, she was trying to make a living. It's easy to blame Desdemona. Ken, her ex-partner should have taken more responsibility.'

I thought of how Sarah was criticised for not being good enough for Samuel Coleridge while she juggled bringing up children with very little money in their tiny cottage.

'I have been going through things with Desdemona,' Dora said, 'trying to help her come to terms with what happened. As I think you know, Cassio had a stutter – especially when he got stressed – and it seemed to get worse when he got to his teenage years. She persuaded him to try some drugs, and it worked. His stuttering went and he suddenly appeared more confident.'

'An unconventional cure,' said Jonathan, 'but his stutter put him at a terrible disadvantage.'

'I have heard tales of him being bullied at school,' said Dora. 'The problem was, his relief from the stutter only lasted as long as he was taking the drugs. Then, of course, he became addicted and wanted more, but he really didn't have enough money from his part-time café job. Some cash that Desdemona kept in the house went missing. There was a big row and, of course, he went missing.'

'We think what happened then is that he got hold of some ketamine,' said Jonathan. 'It's much cheaper than cocaine or heroin but the doses are very variable. People don't always know what they are taking.'

'The Inspector said it's become an epidemic,' continued Dora. 'Every single day someone dies from an overdose of ketamine.'

'I'm so sorry that his life had to end like that. It's difficult not to put some measure of the blame on Desdemona.'

'The truth is she blames herself. She was trying to help - in her own eccentric way.'

We did manage to talk of other things over lunch, mainly Coleridge and Wordsworth things, forthcoming events at The Coleridge Society - and the bookshop. Despite the difficulty of the situation, I was very comfortable in their company and invited them to visit the bookshop and stay with me. Beneath the surface, though, my brain was always re-evaluating what had happened to Cassio and Desdemona's part in this. I heard Esther's moderating voice in my head. I had planned to return home in the afternoon but felt I had unfinished business.

'I have one more favour to ask,' I said to Dora. 'Or at least to ask your advice. I wondered if I could visit Dedemona?'

I think my request took her by surprise.

'Why, yes I suppose that's possible.'

I explained my reasons.

She rang Desdemona and luckily found her in.

As I stood on the threshold of her cottage, we both hesitated before she flung her arms around me in a warm embrace.

'I'm so sorry,' she said.

'No, I'm sorry for Cassio,' I said as tears fell from my eyes.

'Jonathan and Dora have been telling me about Cassio,' I said. 'I felt it would help me if I knew more.'

'I'll make some tea, unless you want anything stronger.'

'No, tea's fine. I'll be driving back later.'

There was a line of photos, all including Cassio, spread around a table.

'He's a handsome boy,' I said, not yet ready to use the past tense for someone who had died so recently.

'Yes, I've been collecting photos. I feel I need to have him around me. I'm not ready to give up on him yet.'

'Yes, of course.'

'We were very close, though we argued a lot. He was a lonely child. I was his friend as well as his mother, but I was always very busy and was not able to give him as much time as I wanted. We were also very isolated where we lived at the time. When his father left things became very difficult – not that he was much good when he was here.'

'It must have been a difficult thing to cope with.'

'He did love his films and books. When he discovered one he was really interested in he would come down and talk for hours to me. A monologue, not a conversation – and not a single stutter. It's what they call a *talk alone* effect even though he wasn't technically alone with me. If I interrupted, though, that's when he stuttered. And it got much worse when he was at school or talking to other people.'

There was a long exhalation of breath.

'You have probably heard I dabble in drugs. But I'm not an addict, not like Coleridge. I mostly smoke hashish for a condition I have. I snorted some heroine to mimic the experience that Coleridge had writing "Kubla Khan" on a couple of occasions.

'I know it was probably wrong of me, but I thought it might help Cassio. And it did… except he got addicted. I just wanted him to be able to relax so he didn't stutter. He started getting it from someone at the café who supplied the stuff. Before I knew it, he had become addicted to morphine and cocaine. The trouble is, it's so expensive. He couldn't afford it on his wages at the café. He even stole from me. That's what drug addiction does to you. And then he got hold of some ketamine. It's sometimes difficult to judge the doses you've been given or what it's been mixed with. He went to sleep and never woke up.'

'I'm so sorry…'

She bent forward and looked like she was going to collapse into a heap. We both ended up on our knees on the floor. I held her.

'You mustn't blame yourself. You did what you thought would help.'

I could not believe the words that were coming out of my mouth after my earlier comments to Esther, but I felt they were right. I made some more tea and cut a piece of lemon drizzle cake that Dora had provided.

'Dora's so kind,' said Desdemona through her tears as we both ate the cake and slurped tea. 'I didn't realise how hungry I was.'

We both sat there quietly for a few moments.

'I hope you don't mind me asking,' I said, at last. 'But why do you think Cassio attacked me?'

'He thought you were carrying *Lyrical Ballads*. Again, my fault. He was in the midst of his addiction. I kept trying to get him interested, hoping to get him to come to the talks and hear my reading. Dora had told me how much it was worth. I shouldn't have told Cassio. He sold things on the internet, films and books he had finished with. I guess that was what he had planned, to get money for his addiction.'

'Part of me almost wishes I did have *Lyrical Ballads* on me to steal, then he wouldn't have got hold of that ketamine.'

'We don't know that really. I just wish I could have got him some professional help.'

When I arrived home, I could not settle. I rang Esther and explained about my visit.

'You did the right thing,' she said. 'I'm proud of you.'

'I did it because of you – and Dora.'

'She was doing what she thought was right by helping him with his stutter. It's difficult for us to understand how much he was affected by that and what a relief it was to be free from it, however briefly. It's such a shame that he became addicted and had that rogue dose.'

'Another Somerset tragedy. But despite everything, you know, I don't regret my visit. I have made new friends.'

'And friendship is so important.'

'We've been through so much together in this last year. You know I was wondering if we …'

I was about to ask Esther if we may move towards a closer friendship with all that entailed but, at that moment, I saw another call was coming through.'

I considered ignoring it, but Esther had sensed something.

'What is it?' she said.

'Oh, it's just my mother trying to get through.'

'Better get it. It might be important. In any case, I have to go and feed the chickens, and I have a ton of other things to do.'

She finished the call.

The moment had passed.

'Hello, mother,' I said.

Acknowledgements

Special thanks to my wife Jo for once again putting me straight on the plot and ironing out inconsistencies at an early stage (and for putting up with me!) Thanks also to my sister Vivienne for being my proof reader and copy editor. I can't thank you enough for all the hours you have put in.

I am grateful to the friends and family members who have accompanied me on various stages of my own walk along The Coleridge Way, and to the 'drivers' who have got me to start and pick-up points. Your companionship and interest in my project have been very much appreciated.

Thank you very much to The Friends of Coleridge who have recently put on a number of events that I have attended and which have given me much rich source material for my book.

Thanks are also due to the Quantock Poetry Trail Group led by Ralph Hoyte who is responsible for the poetry app mentioned in the story. I would particularly like to mention Anne Lovejoy, Rachel Irven and Angela Wensley who I accompanied on a poetry walk (along with others) and who showed me how to use the poetry app. Extra thanks to Angela, who took me on a targeted walk whose purpose was to use some of the material in my book. As a result, I used one of Angela's poems "Views From Walford's Gibbet" and also Jan Martin's poem "Walford's Gibbet". These poems and all the poems written by the Quantock Poetry Trail Group can be seen at: https://quantockpoetrytrail. uk/maps-2/the-poets/

Jan Martin's poetry collections *We Are Here Between, Behind the Veil* and *Woods, Ways and Waters*, and Anne Lovejoy's *Memory Box* are available, among other places, from Brendon Books, Bath Place, Taunton.

There are a wide variety of biographies on the Coleridges and Wordsworths. For me, the bible was Richard Holmes two volume series, *Early Visions* and *Darker Reflections*. I also found very useful Tom Mayberry's *Wordsworth in the West Country*. Two books by Molly Lefebure: *The Bondage of Love: A Life of Mrs. Samuel Taylor Coleridge* and *Samuel Taylor Coleridge: A Bondage* of

Opium I found particularly insightful.

Finally, I would like to thank members of the United Reform Church in Taunton and also and members of The Temple Methodist Church who showed me round their beautiful premises and provided me with much valuable information.

The three books in the Elliot Todd Mystery Series, The Shakespeare Thief, Roman Holiday and Somerset Odyssey, should be widely available in print and online. If you have trouble obtaining a copy or would like a signed copy please email your request for the attention of Lionel Ward at brendonbooks@gmail.com Please leave reviews from where you purchased the book or on review sites and feel free to give comments or feedback to lionelward1@gmail.com

www.ingramcontent.com/pod-product-compliance
Lightning Source LLC
Chambersburg PA
CBHW020008140726
47904CB00018B/2126